MW01093216

Pansflorawood

by J.J. Adams

This book is a work of fiction. Names, characters, places and incidents are either the product of the author's imagination or are used fictionally. Any resemblance to actual persons, living or dead, or to actual events or locales is entirely coincidental.

This book is licensed for your personal enjoyment only. This book may not be re-sold or given away to other people. If you like to share this book with another person, please purchase an additional copy for each person you share it with.

Copyright 2021 J. J. Adams. All rights reserved. Including the right to reproduce this book or portions thereof in any form. No part of this text may be reproduced in any form without the express written permission of the author.

This book is dedicated to my parents,
for teaching me love is the key that
unlocks the heart to happiness.

Table of Contents

CHAPTER 1

Hornbuckle and Honeysuckle

A single forest faun sits on a petrified tree stump playing his panpipes. He is half stag, half boy, with tan skin and short curly dark brown hair. Out of a nearby Evergreen Tree flies an orange and black Butterfly girl with long red hair and big delicate wings. She encircles the laughing faun tickling him in a shower of shimmering stardust.

The butterfly fairy calls out to him, "Forest faun! It's the dawn! Forest faun, it's been too long! Hornbuckle now come on! It is the time when the bells will chime to find the briar baskets under the Juniper Pine." She twinkles on and off toward a thick forest of towering trees.

Hornbuckle stops playing, stands up and gallops quickly following behind the Butterfly Fairy far off into the woods yelling back, "Honeysuckle, wait for me, I do not wish to fall behind you see!"

Hornbuckle sees Honeysuckle in the distance weaving in and out of the massive mounds covered in green grass. Trotting as fast as he can to catch up with her, he looks around to see a vast woodland of Evergreen Pines surrounding them. The fast-moving faun watches the twinkling fairy as she finally stops by a bubbling brook that streams out into a pristine pond flowing into a large lake filled with blooming blossoms of Lotus Lilies.

Honeysuckle smiles as she sees a family of swimming swans crossing the water with their feathery chicklings. The fairy flutters down digging inside an ivy-covered treehouse sitting at the base of a giant Juniper Pine. Honeysuckle turns toward the frowning faun smiling, "Here is your basket Hornbuckle of purple grape and vine, this pink Wisteria one, well of course this one is mine."

She hands him his grapevine covered basket as she clutches hers in her hands, "To the Lotus Lily I will go to get her mauve crystal stone, you will find his indigo one in the grotto though you must go alone." She points at the misty mountain far off in the distance and giggles softly.

Hornbuckle smiles at her as he grabs his wicker weaved basket picking off one of the purple grapes to eat. He turns around to see a hundred-foot waterfall cascading down the side of the steep emerald green mountain. He begins to briskly make his way around the large lake toward the crashing falls.

Honeysuckle yells out, "You must follow the path of the Blue Angel Morning Glories as they fold to sleep, they will lead you to the inside of Crystalline Cavern dark and deep!"

Honeysuckle swiftly flitters away to the largest Lotus Lily in the fish filled pond. She sees the sparkling stone in the radiant sunlight gleaming brightly from within an open flower. Flying closer to the perfect pink crystal it glitters more brilliantly inside the center of a pale pink lotus. She hovers over the lovely lily carefully scooping out the mauve crystal with both hands. She admires the view of the many water lilies and waves to the Snapdragonflies before she flies back to place it inside the briar basket.

Fluttering around through the many different shrubs and trees she looks everywhere for Hornbuckle. Realizing he is nowhere to be found the fragile fairy glides gracefully onto a big branch covered in an ivy vine to wait and listen for him. She makes herself a chair from the ivy leaves overlooking the weeds and wildflowers sitting at the top of the giant Juniper.

Hornbuckle gallops his way across a field of Periwinkle plants then through a Cornflowers crop that surrounds the base of the misty mountain. The long-overgrown vines of Morning Glories weave through a wide Hawthorn hedge growing on each side of his path.

As he makes his way along the pathway the hundreds of flowers all close like a folding fan in synchronicity. Leading him to the mouth of the mountain he slowly walks around cautiously. He precedes to pass slowly under a crashing waterfall splashing over the granite rocks above him creating a rushing river.

Hornbuckle finds the small opening to the cave as he steps through a jagged doorway of brown boulders into an underground tunnel of Hexagonal Quartzite twisting around inside the cold cavern. He walks down a narrow path following it farther down into the dark, dank tunnel. Finally seeing the blue glowing light of dancing rays above him he follows it to find its reflection from off of a crystal-clear pool. The giant white slabs of large quartz clusters shoot out from the walls creating prisms of rainbows. The only light source for him to see inside the dimly lit cavern was the sunset sunbeams reflecting within a few of the clear crystals lighting up the rock room.

Stepping closer to the pool he carefully approaches the still water where a vivid violet beam emanates from the indigo crystal. The mystical crystal is wedged into a Black Basalt alter at the edge of the transparent pool disguised as a regular rock. Hornbuckle reaches in the shallow water to pull out the gleaming gem that unexpectedly illuminates the darkness with a bluish-purple light. He stares at it in awe as the crystal sparkles in its multifaceted cut, clarity and color before he places it inside the basket.

Hornbuckle turns around quickly and moves back through the long pathway to exit back out the opening of Crystalline Cavern. Hurrying back under the waterfall he runs past the sleeping Morning Glories and into the Cornflower crop. He looks around for a certain Juniper Pine covered in ivy. Running along through the flower field he sees the faint glow of warm incandescence imitating candlelight emanating from Honeysuckle. Her small sparkle lights up the darkness from where she sits on the twig of the Evergreen tree as the sun fades. Dusk has arrived as the sun fades on the horizon turning the clouds bright pink against a dark purple sky.

"I hear the music Hornbuckle they are approaching, now we must go," She picks up her briar basket, "We don't want to be late for the sacred ceremony you know?"

Honeysuckle speeds off into the fern forest with dense pines as Hornbuckle runs behind her following through the dark woods below. The dirt pathway is lit up by bioluminescent bugs skipping by in the unfurling fiddles under the sprawling Sycamores, Spruce and Sequoia trees. Floating fireflies' glow on and off through the thick woodland as they both dash in and out the bushes. The last rays of the sun shine down in golden lines of light through the canopy of leaves hanging above.

Honeysuckle and Hornbuckle soon meet up together inside a mossy meadow full of willows and weeds. The smell of fragrant flowers permeates the air from all the handmade wreaths, bouquets and archways that decorate the doorways and tables. The faun and fairy walk to the center of the wide-open fairy ring inside a circle of Toadstool Mushrooms. The fairy ring is lit up by the friendly fireflies holding flower lanterns over stone carved tables and chairs filled with flowers.

The are greeted by the mythical creatures and creepy critters seated at the other tables and chairs within the many mushrooms. The family and friends of Flora Fae Fairies and Fauna Wood Elves have come to join together for the celestial celebration. The gathered guests from the other homes and hives living inside this forgotten forest choose an empty table or chair to sit in as they arrive.

Honeysuckle descends down to meet Hornbuckle in the center of the mushroom circle. As he watches her flutter fly next to him, they both sit down together in Opal stone chairs seated at each side of the Rosewood platform stage adorned in cobweb curtains. Growing in the mossy meadow there is a colorful variety of bright, blooming blossoms dancing in the breeze.

CHAPTER 2

Camellia and Obsidian

In the distance the sound of music becomes louder and louder as the Flora Fae Fairies and Fauna Wood Elves parade out of the forest playing on fern fiddles and blowing on Angel Trumpets. They gracefully pass by tooting Reed Root flutes and ringing Bonnie Bluebells. The fairies and elves dance out over the fields of Lavender and Lilacs across the mossy meadow and into the fairy ring. They are all dressed in leaves, twigs, flowers, feathers and fine fabrics. They mix different berries and clays together to make up their coffee and cream complexions. Already seated at the main table are Obsidian and Camellias' parents, they wait calmly while smiling and waving at many familiar faces.

The smell of Night Blooming Jasmine mixed with wet rain fills the air with perfume. Obsidians mother Lady Hydrangea closes her eyes while inhaling the sweet scent smiling. A dark shadow quickly darts from left to right above the wed-binding venue. By the time her husband Lord Feldspar looks up in the sky to see what it was he observes only a small group of Snapdragonflies soaring over the entire fairy ring throwing tiny white rose petals.

Feldspar shakes his head stating to his wife, "I must be going batty; I could have sworn the shadow was bigger than that."

Hydrangea reassures Lord Feldspar, "It's just the Snapdragonflies in formation, flying over to roll out the welcome mat."

Flora Fae Fairies and Fauna Wood Elves continue to play upon their harmonious harps, flutes and trumpets while ringing their wind chimes of Bluebells.

Camellia, The Lady of the Light and Obsidian, the Lord of the Night appear at the entrance of an archway covered in fruits and flowers.

The Lord and Lady smile at each other before joining arms as the handsome elf escorts his beautiful bride past numerous sandstone tables with many excited guests staring silently. The couple walk slowly, arm in arm toward the Rosewood stage in rhythm with the melodious music.

Lord Obsidian is dressed in a dark purple silk shirt with jet black pants, ink-stained boots and a hooded cloak. A silver crown shines like a crescent moon in his long midnight hair. Lady Camellia is dressed in a gown of glittering gold decorated with pale pink roses and a dazzling crown of Opal Borealis crystals that sparkle like sunlight in her long, honey hair. A Harvest Moon has begun to rise in the sky as the rays of rainbow colors fade into the violet twilight.

Hornbuckle and Honeysuckle stand up and approach the couple with their wicker weaved briar baskets. Honeysuckle places the wisteria basket on a Moonstone table next to Camellia. Hornbuckle places the grapevine basket on a separate Moonstone table next to Obsidian. Both tables have one, three-pronged silver candelabra standing with unlit white taper candles placed inside. The wed-binding couple are holding hands as they proceed up the stairs together onto the wooden platform stage where everyone can see them. As they both turn to face each other Bleeding Heart flower lanterns shine a crimson color on their faces. The lanterns sway above them in the soft blowing breeze. The audience applauds while watching with wide eyes of anticipation at stage illuminated in soft pink and rosy red.

Hundreds of flickering fireflies gather together uniting to form one bright spotlight over the center of the fairy ring. Hornbuckle jumps out into the center announcing, "Welcome Ladybirds! Gentlebugs! As well as all blessed beasts big and small, to our long-awaited wed-binding on this Equinox of Fall! In this enchanted garden of Pansflorawood Glen an awakening shall now begin! We thank you all for arriving here, in the Autumn evening this time of year! In this sacred circle we come in celebration of this joining of hearts in jolly jubilation!"

The audience clap and cheers as Camellias father, Topaz Rosetree stands up before walking over to the stage to hand the binding broom to Hornbuckle. The broom is decorated with Autumn leaves, pinecones and acorns as the flushing faun bows accepting it graciously.

Feldspar walks up next after him to pass Honeysuckle the sparkling silver scarf from his outstretched arms while she bows taking it from him then bringing over to Hornbuckle.

The faun and fairy both turn to Obsidian and Camellia on the stage, Hornbuckle gives the happy couple the binding broom. Obsidian and Camellia reach out to hold the handle of the broom with their left hands. Hornbuckle proceeds to tie the silver scarf around the wrists of the Lord and Lady fastening their hands to bond with the binding broom.

Hornbuckle looks at Camellia with a happy-go-lucky grin then turns his head toward Obsidian, "Lady of the Light, Lord of the Night, we give love for our Mother Earth, as her axis is spun, when she gives birth. Let this binding broom stand as two becomes one. When two hearts intertwined in unison. Gaia's grace is a promise to perform the protection for each other come rain, wind, snow or storm. Do you Obsidian Jasperstone take Camellia Rosetree as your own, to share your heart, hearth, hill and home?"

Obsidian looks deep into the golden eyes of his beautiful bride-to-be, "With a binding broom our love shall bloom, as I focus my mind's eye to guard, guide, protect and instruct you as the time goes by. I bind you to be mine from now until the end of time, becoming one in unison as we wed-bind."

Hornbuckle turns to face Camellia, "The moon is dim, while the sun is bright. Your wisdom reflects both the dark and the light. The moon will conceal what the sun will reveal between the dawn and the dusk twilight. The clock ticks the tock of time that intertwines your mind as your hearts wed-bind. Do you Camellia Rosetree take Obsidian Jasperstone to be your one and only for merely you alone?"

The beautiful bride turns her head to look at her betrothed beloved, staring lovingly into Obsidian's intense dark eyes, "With a binding broom our love shall bloom as I focus my mind's eye to guard, guide, protect and instruct you as the time goes by. I bind you to be mine from now until the end of time, becoming one in unison as we wed-bind."

Hornbuckle unties the silver scarf releasing the couples previously bound hands and taking the binding broom out of couples' grasp.

Honeysuckle walks over to the center of the fairy ring meeting with a Saffron Salamander Dragon holding out two taper candles. He uses his fiery breath to light them both up before handing them to her. One candle is light pink and the other is dark purple. The fire from the dancing candlelight brightens up her smiling face as she turns to head back to stand on the Rosewood stage.

Hornbuckle picks up another non-lit white candle out of the candelabra.

Honeysuckle gives the pink candle to Camellia while giving the purple candle to Obsidian at the same time.

Hornbuckle holds the broom up with one hand while holding the candle between the two lovers with the other. "Let this flame be a symbol of our Father Sky that watches us yearly with his sun's eye. A bright light to warm up any cold stormy night. We wed-bind this Lord and Lady with the skies silver moon and Earth's binding broom!"

Hornbuckle proceeds to point the wooden handle upward at the glowing floating orb while holding the white candle out between the wed-binding couple. He looks at each of them, one then the other, "Our Elven Lord Obsidian Jasperstone, that makes Weeping Willow Hollow his home, wed-binding tonight with the lovely Lady of the Light from the lush land of Luneria, a star stunning sight. May you both be the twin flames of each other from your soul's eternal past, within the eternity of time where your love shall infinitely last!"

Obsidian and Camellia use their separate candle flames to ignite the white candle Hornbuckle is holding. The couple now take the lit white candle with their left hands and exchange the purple and pink ones with the forest faun. He hands Honeysuckle the binding broom before taking one candle in each hand, blows them out, then hands them over to Honeysuckle who sets them both down on the table top.

Hornbuckle closes his eyes and lowers his head speaking sternly, "On this face the hands unwind that disperse the tones of time. Two become one as they recite the rhymes, in rhythm with the riddle when the clock chimes. When the hourglass sends sands sifting, seeds of Mother Earth and Father Sky stay shifting. May they bless this husband and wife, in the symbiotic cycle within the circle of life. This one flame represents the twin flames of you two coming together to unite both of you."

Camellia and Obsidian continue to recite the ritual of the ancient ceremony holding the one white candle with their left hands together, "Rays of rainbows firing into a spiraling symphony of supernatural stardust send comets crisscrossing the cosmos in light flares that brightly bust. As we are all connected to life force we are protected by this source, the natural law is just. The moon reflects the sun's rays contrasting the fire of desire that is endless and everlasting."

Honeysuckle takes the white candle away from the happy couple blowing it out before placing it back down on the tabletop. A Nature Nymph comes dancing through the crowd like a blue ballerina holding a silver chalice in each of her hands. Honeysuckle flitters down to greet the Flora Fae Fairy, taking both chalices from her. Honeysuckle turns to flutter fly back over to Camellia handing one chalice to her and the other to Obsidian. The Lord and Lady interlock arms holding up each chalice while smiling at each other.

Many sparking stars shine directly above the mushroom circle illuminating the fairy ring in a pale luminescence.

Hornbuckle nods looking over at Obsidian and then at Camellia, "Here is the soul spring water to drink together as your minds intertwine and your hearts wed-bind. With this magical silver chalice may you unite his castle and her palace. Where you both shall rule together with all animals, bees, bugs and birds of a feather."

Obsidian and Camellia drink from their chalices at the same time gazing into each other's eyes speaking as one, "Endurance like water brings us strength and comfort to cleanse as the psychic subconscious of our intuition blends. We are lovers as well as best friends, feeling our love in this life never ends. We will have many children; cherub angels appear to celebrate seasons by the cycle of the year. We shall live our lives without any regret, like the clouds that drip rain where dewdrops are set."

Camellia hands Obsidian her chalice as he hands her his; they drink again while facing each other, "I bind you to my heart, I bind you to my mind, we're soulmates in unison as we wed-bind."

They interlock arms putting their chalice up to the others lips letting their partner drink the last of the spring water. The couple hand their chalices to Hornbuckle who places them down on the nearby table. Hornbuckle picks up the grapevine basket as Honeysuckle takes her Wisteria basket walking toward the Lord and Lady. They both eagerly look into their baskets to see their geometric gems glittering brilliantly in the lantern light.

Honeysuckle continues to hold the basket for Camellia as she reaches down to cup her mauve crystal with both hands. Obsidian reaches inside his to wrap his long fingers around the indigo crystal. They continue to stare at each other while holding out the mystical crystals with their right hands pointed up at the Harvest Moon. They touch the two crystals together which sends radiant rainbows firing off into every direction.

The lovers embrace in the shooting stars of passing prisms with each of their left arms holding the other by the waist.

Hornbuckle looks skyward while lifting up both his arms, "These healing crystals hold the universal laws in place, brought here long ago by the Star Sisters of space. The secret mystery of ancient history connects Lady Camellia and Lord Obsidian into the divine plan, becoming one in unison between this woman and this man. Mother Earth shall give birth, Father Sky will kiss the sea, as it is, as it was, as it always shall be, an enigma of eternity. Your internal universe into the external multiverse will connect and protect you through, as you vow to keep your souls pure and true devoted only to each other. This is what you promise to do?"

Camellia places her crystal with her right hand into Obsidian's left hand. He gives her his crystal with his right hand into her open left palm. They both grasp the powerful crystals once again touching the sacred stones together.

Together the couple says, "Our hearts, souls and minds intertwine as we fuse with the divine uniting to wed-bind. You shall be mine from now until the end of time."

Obsidian glances up at the two crystals before locking eyes with Camellia again, "Uniting your mauve crystal with my indigo stone, will connect our twin flames together to be only yours alone. A wed-binding spell winding promise under a starlit sky, to guard, guide, protect and instruct you as the time goes by. I vow to be true my love, I do."

Teardrops form in Camellia's eyes as they fall slowly down her fair face. She softly touches Obsidian's cheek with her right hand, "Uniting your indigo crystal with my mauve stone, will connect our twin flames together to be only yours alone. A wed-binding spell winding promise under a starlit sky, to guard, guide, protect and instruct you as the time goes by. I vow to be true my love, I do."

Obsidian and Camellia chant once again in unison, "Here in this enchanted garden of Pansflorawood Glen, energy flows where attention goes, our life together shall now begin. I bind you to my heart, I bind you to my mind, so that we never part as two hearts intertwined. Becoming one in unison as we wed-bind. I vow to be true, my love, I do."

Hornbuckle yells out to the audience loudly, "I now give you Obsidian and Camellia Jasperstone! Two became one, as it should be; leaders of Luneria, in the crystal Kingdom by the sea! As Greenman of the Glen shall bless us once again! You may now kiss each other to unite the Lady of the Light with the Lord of the Night, under a special spell winding, this celebration of wed-binding! Thank you all for witnessing tonight, with this sky filled with starlit moonlight!"

Hornbuckle takes the crystal from Obsidian's hand while Honeysuckle reaches to grab the other crystal from the blushing bride.

Obsidian kisses Camellia passionately as all the guests clap and cheer. Camellias' mother, Zinnia Rosetree takes the family heirloom out from under her green velvet cloak. It's a sparkling Lightning Wand made out of pure Opal Borealis Crystal. Once Camellia takes possession of it in her hand, she holds it skyward as powerful prisms of light flash in all directions.

Lady Hydrangea hands Obsidian their family heirloom at the same time. The Thunder Sword made of Amethyst and silver steel having a sharp shiny Titanium edge. The dark elf puts the jewel encrusted sword into his engraved metal sheath attaching it to his leather belt. The fairy bride and elf groom take their baskets with them as they walk over to a Moonstone Marble table. They place both baskets on a fruit and flower alter made from a young budding Birch Tree behind it.

The crowds of creatures, insects and woodland animals laugh and cheer as they dance to the various musical instruments performed by the rest of the fairies and elves. Their mystical melodies echoing throughout the mossy meadow, tall trees and flower fields.

"Miracle!" The creatures and critters cry out joyfully.

A parade of iridescent blue and purple Snapdragonflies speed over Lady Camellia and Lord Obsidian dropping tiny pastel petals.

The two lovers nod to their gathered guests as they walk around to sit in the middle of a long table. The Flora Fae and Fauna Wood court stand to greet them as they bow, clap and cheer. Smiling and laughing the Lord and Lady sit down to join the others to enjoying their families, friends and food.

All of the tables are set with delicate dishes, clear glasses, silverware and wooden bowls. The large long tables are filled with mashed mint potatoes, mushrooms in acorn sauce, turnip soup and Kale herb salad. There are apple and peach jams and jellies with candied nut tarts and citrus fruits piled on the plates. The glasses contain Natural Nectar, Camellia's personal favorite. Two three-tiered carrot cakes covered in mulberries, boysenberries and raspberries sit at the center of each dinner table.

Camellia and Obsidian walk over to cut each cake on every table before passing it out on leaf dishes to their grateful guests. The fairies and elves sit down to eat at tables set with pink and purple roses and decorated in fabulous fabrics. Their faces are lit up by the shinning chandeliers that swing above in the trees. Flower wreaths and floral bouquets adorn the make shift walls of marvelous material.

Hornbuckle whistles an upbeat tune through his panpipes while the crowd eats, talks and drinks together.

A Black Witch Moth with eyes painted on the back of its wings pours Elderberry Wine into Camellia and Obsidian's silver chalices. The large moth flutters along to fill the other guests' chalices with Elderberry wine.

Hornbuckle blows a loud tone through his panpipes getting everyone to look up and become silent. He jumps out into the middle of centerstage exclaiming, "Welcome Ladybirds, Gentlebugs and all Blessed Beasts here within Pansflorawood Glen! We are proud to present the *Birds of Paradise* for an extravaganza to begin! They have come to perform this night about the desires and dishonors of men! Story telling knowing wrong from right of who, where, why and when! For every year in this meadow here, we celebrate the wed-binding of our new Queen and King, uniting us all together inside this fairy ring! To gather amongst these toadstools to play music, dance and sing! On this October Eve in this sacred space, we shall dress our Fairy Queen in a gown of silk spun lace. This evening, after the *Birds of Paradise* performance, our Lord and Lady will have their first dance!"

Honeysuckle flies out from a nearby red and white polka dotted mushroom encircling Hornbuckle. Floating gently down to stand beside him she sings in a high-pitched voice, "You will find blooming Jasmine in the night under Snowdrop lantern light, sensually enhancing the fragrant smell to guide our way, anytime of day, to the Moonstone wishing well. Entering a mother of pearl palace that the Lord and Lady will share, surrounded by sturdy stables for unicorns and white winged mare. Taking long strolls past grassy knolls down to an old windmill winding snail trail. You will find them kissing on a honeybee hive or dancing together midair, in her glowing gossamer gown barely there. Lay our lovely lady down to sleep in a flower bed of roses red, with soft petal pillows to place her head. While she sleeps in silent slumber within her cobweb cocoon, surrounded by fragrant flowers for your happy honeymoon. When her beloved comes to join her, a soprano song we'll sing of sonata sonnets for our faithful Queen and King!"

Honeysuckle spins upward around and around sending glittering golden pollen dust into the air creating a sparkling spiral. Hornbuckle begins Fauna Folk dancing beneath her singing, "As our Lord and Lady awake from their cobweb cocoon, we will make meals for them under a crescent moon. Satyrs shall smash grapes for hours while centaurs play pan pipes in the flowers. The wisdom of antiquity is softly spoken through every tree. Upon the Ash, Oak and Evergreen with Weeping Willows wailing scream. Amidst the faint fireflies' glow with food, drink, song and dance where thespian birds put on a show! Here they will perform tonight for our united Queen and King, with a symphony of music inside this fairy ring! A place of musical lyric mixed with fine art, will put us all in rhythm to follow our heart!" Once more, the forest faun plays his pan pipes.

Honeysuckle flutters softly down into the center circle to sing, "I ride upon the silky swan holding tightly to her wings, as we glide upon the Lotus Lake through waterfalls and springs. This is the valley of the Leprechauns, Imps and Nut Gnomes, who make the giant trees and tiny mushrooms here their homes. Clovers and cherries attract elves and fairies, as well as flowers, fruits, nuts and berries. You can spot them sitting on an ivy vine or flying together mid-air, feeding the forest creatures of deer, squirrel, fox and hare. In this mossy meadow of Pansflorawood Glen, it's merry May meeting once upon a time again. We shall all gather here next year in sunny Spring, inside this patch of magic mushrooms known as a fairy ring."

Hornbuckle pipes up, "A Solstice celebration to make wishes come true, at first sunrise when the sky turns bright blue. Where we wish into the wishing well, as only time will tell, to grant a wish come true for you, a captivating spell. We weave a dream of fantasy with every song we sing, so let's welcome the *Birds of Paradise* here, to perform now for our Queen and King!"

The butterfly fairy smiles while waving at the flushing faun. Honeysuckle and Hornbuckle sit back down on their Opal stone chairs watching and waiting.

Creatures and critters clap and cheer as more fireflies come together to brighten up their spotlight. The Flora Fae Fairies and Fauna Wood Elves tune down their Bonnie Bluebells and turn off their white Snowdrop Jasmine lanterns.

CHAPTER 3

Hawaiian Phoenix

Large Black Boars beat loudly on Polynesian Ipu drums made of hollowed out giant gourds. Thick fog forms reflecting an image of a live volcano with lava pouring into the ocean creating steam. In the distance the Hawaiian Phoenix emerges as flickering flames of fire. The many watching eyes of the creatures and critters see a stunning flaming Firebird now standing elegantly beneath the fireflies' spotlight. Ember has long red feathers around her waist that look like waving grass. Her feet are like spun gold, Flame flowers adorn her head feathers.

The Hawaiian Phoenix sings, "I am a glowing Ember this is my name, a flowing amber guardian of the flame. A volcano goddess of liquid fires sparks molten formations from creative desires. Will you offer me a lei of colored rainbows for my hair? In the Garden of the Gods, where I make my home there. When magma intruders ignite in ashes I emerge as your cinder friend, born from the core of the Earth where time and space have no end. Blazes that burn, then consumes, a maze of jet black, tunnel tombs. I protect my gardens of every art color shade, all of my creations from my caldera that I've made. Vulcan in knowledge, with wisdom in vapor, security is solid for Mother Earth in nature. Come with me to the mermaid's cove, where pirates have buried a treasure trove with a white sandy beach and a coconut grove. We shall swim with the dolphins in the sea at the Pili Grass hut, a sacred space in harmony. I will welcome our evening by blowing a big Conch Shell, then listen to shore nesting birds that have a tale to tell. We shall feast at dawn then dance to sway to the drumbeat of dusk at end of the day. I will give you a black pearl in an oyster from the sea, calling my mariner man to bring him back to me. The *Birds of Paradise* are so happy here, since we celebrate the seasons every year. From lush foliage down to jet black boulders, steam of smoke from fissures smolders. For the message from out of the cinder crater is to learn the wisdom to nurture nature." Ember dances Hula while waving her large feathers in the shining spotlight.

Moving her body in front of all the guests she tells her story. Gracefully she glides over to perform directly before Lady Camellia and Lord Obsidian singing sweetly, "Lagoons here are a crescent shape of deep turquoise blue set on black sand beaches with palm trees all weaved through. The jagged jungle becomes wet with rain dripping like a fountain, from tops of craggy cliff sides cascading down the mountain. I fly from the center of a steaming crater down past ebony lava rope trails, swim inside the ocean with blue dolphins and gray whales. Painting perfect pictures in fern grottos of every art color hue, all the land and sea that I must create to do. Sealed in time, written on paper, the power source of pure life force that permeates in nature."

Ember dances around the fairy ring spinning as the flames of her feathers lick up into the air higher and higher, "Microorganisms spin a spiral round, giving the galaxy gravity to keep us on the ground. Winding winds by a starry sky at sunset; we are the *Birds of Paradise* you shall never forget. Our valleys are filled with fragrance over field and stream, orchid orchards throughout the lush hills of green. With every bird, bug, bee and bat there is to be seen. A lava lake of liquid fire ignites formations flowing, setting off sparks of fireworks in the night time glowing. I shall be born to rise from ashes then die to be born again, regeneration of reincarnation the beginning is now the end. All of this land from my caldera that I've made, from a torch of flame into a bursting blaze parade! For nurturing all creatures is my stature, love is as solid as a rock, Mother Earth is nature!"

The audience claps loudly and yells out. "Miracle! Miracle!"

Ember continues to dance around inside the fairy ring shining brilliantly like a fox fire. The clapping subsides as she stops and turns back to exit.

Ember quickly spins around to her audience in a solid stance stating, "Leave a legacy that lasts forever and guardian ghosts will leave you never. *Do not reject or neglect her; love, respect and protect her!"* Ember turns in a slow circle before she exits out holding her flaming wings high up into the air.

The creatures and critters all clap and cheer, "Miracle! "Oracle!"

CHAPTER 4

Indian Eagle

A big Brown Bear starts to strike on a large single drum sending a booming beat throughout the trees. Numerous deer ring bells on their antlers walking around along the outside of the lantern lit fairy ring. Emerging from the cobweb curtains a Golden Eagle with a feathered headdress of a native chief and beaded outfit.

He dances out into the spotlight lifting his legs as he sings, "My name is Sage Thunder Cloud; I sing to you strong, proud and loud! A song to cope that's true, open your eyes to hope anew. Thanking Mother Earth, for giving birth, a new awareness of unity and peace. As Gaia's Garden changes wars of hatred will have to cease. Replenish our natural resources so we can breathe to live, harvest our various crops that we can grow and give. The cycle of the food chain is what makes the world go around, to spin the wheel of fortune so that you may hear its sound. A tiny acorn will turn into a mighty Oak as it grows up from the ground. The medicine man has a dream catcher hanging over his head projecting into the astral world, while he sleeps in his tee-pee bed. Giving gifts to equally share with all, the changing seasons of winter, spring, summer and fall. When winter brings families together, then springtime brings lovebirds to call. From falling loose leaves to new fallen snow- If you do not know where you are going, how will you know where to go? Life is a banquet, most hungry where they stand, not seeing the forest through the trees or hearing the sound of the land. Life is a celebration for those who know, the peaceful gentle ways of the Great White Buffalo!"

Sage begins to Pow-wow dance faster while shaking his rain rattle singing, "Thunderbird bring the rain, bring balance back to Mother Earth again! Ancestral spirits, who have gone before show us you're here, open the door! White Buffalo, great bison, in the far plains that you roam, who make this suffering Earth your home. Take away the anger, envy and fears, wipe away the women's tears, creating happiness for children's future years! Within the traveling of time seas to sifting sand, the Great White Buffalo shall live out its life to turn the four colors of man!"

A thick fog surrounds the fairy ring while visions of the White Buffalo are seen running through fields while changing colors from yellow to red then into black. The many guests are mystified as the Golden Eagle with his wide wings outstretched, begins to dance around the circle faster and faster, his rhythm in concert with the loud banging beating drum:

"You are the true bringer of justice worth more than silver or gold; for you bring time to the new and take it from the old. Oh, Great Spirit, hear my prayer- Everywhere in the air. Whose voice carries me with the wind under my wings, let me see the beauty created within all things. Let my hands preserve your lands that I learn honestly to understand. Peace is the inspiration to know the underestimated powers of the Great White Buffalo. I give my gratitude for your existence of birth, from the wise one's message of the beginning of peace on Earth. Focus inward on introspection to have the right perception for timing in perfection. This is the truth of which I sing, with the Great Spirits' blessings that I shall bring. I pray you fall into comfort with ease, growing stronger in the breeze. Father Sun shines his energy in daylight while Mother Moon restores you by star night. Your worries and pain will be washed away by the rain. May you walk gently through the world without struggle or strife, to only know joy every day of your life! When humanity comes together to care the bread basket will be full to share. All of you go walk in peace, for now my song is sung, with every cause, there is an effect, the future has just begun!"

The natives are restless for relevance, ready and roughly relentless. Striving, surviving with all, through seasons of winter, spring, summer and fall. A symbiotic circle spins and swirls around, like a spiral cycle spinning around shooting star bound. A snake with a head full of greed has taken from the crickets who feed. The ladybugs live in the wildflowers and milkweed. Take only from our mothers' milk what you need. I respect and protect my woodland family from every animal, seed and tree. Living life means the world to me. My mighty solar spirit is a warrior star seed!"

Sage lifts up one leg then the other as he dances across the with his wings outstretched, he raises them slowly up to the sun as the light envelops him in a golden glow. He dances around the rim of the fairy ring to the drum beat of the bears as he shakes his rain rattle up at the moon. Sage shakes his body then waves his dark orange brown wings down to stand still into a dark feather cloak.

"Mother Moon makes it rain; Thunderbird kiss the plains again, in a bliss of rains my friend. From the cloud castles and clifftops to rainbow rays on rooftops. A blessing of bountiful harvest you desire created by Earth, air, water and fire. Your intention you decree everything is for the best, turns the karmic compass pointing a path North, East, South and West."

"If you want a future for you and me, you must nurture nature, go outside, plant a tree. Plant corn, beans and squash together with all birds of a feather that flock here together. The beauty of balance in happy harmony with your family joining our loved ones, be a wise one, save a bee. When the wars of hatred finally cease, the planet will be a place of peace. The changing of the seasons has come at last to take us into the future, the present and the past." The beat of the drums becomes louder and faster as Sage bounces up and down to the upbeat rhythm showing off his giant talons.

"Now I hope you understand why the Great White Buffalo changed the four colors of man. We are all one under the sun rotating on this blue ball. Connected and protected by the universal law of truth, freedom and justice for all."

Sage turns to exit out the cobweb curtains as the audience clap and cheer from behind him, "Miracle!"

CHAPTER 5

Chinese Parrot

A red fox plucks at a single Zither Guitar, while rabbits play on two string violins and three cranes play bamboo flutes. Hummingbirds move many wind chimes. A mustard yellow Chinese Parrot wearing a long, shiny satin dress flaps her wings approaching the center of the fairy ring. Thick fog projects the image of a gigantic Aztec Pyramid Temple surrounded by massive mountains at night.

"Good evening, everyone, my name is Peony Sweet Pea, I have come to sing for the Lord and Lady. Long ago an Aztec empire was forged in a valley under a mountain of fire. Where two young lovers were given their destiny to be separated because of jealousy. Her name was Rosa, his name was Jade- He told her *Do not be afraid*' as he cut out tangled brush with his blade. When both realized they would not be free, together fled further into the jungle to flee. They went in search of a Wood Witch for protection and advice, to disguise Rosa so she would not be a sacrifice. Deep into the dark, dense foliage the two lovers came, past the thick plants and misty mountains cloud kissed by the rain. They went into the Banyan Forest sitting by a large calm lake, filled with black swans, big toads, turtles and a snake. Out of a gnarled Banyan Tree came the wood witch who asked them, *What is your plea?*' Jade replied, *We wish to be disguised, so that we can both be free.*' With gems, geodes, sticks and stones she did a spell in a circle of salt and bones. She waves her holly wand around them three times, ringing bells and whistles, waving charms with chimes. The couple transform slowly into jaguars, big, black and sleek as they made off into the jungle with a bloodcurdling shriek!"

Peony dances slowly around the fairy ring using her feathers like fans to hide her face. The pretty parrot glows golden in the fireflies' spotlight softly singing, "Under a spell of the full Harvest Moon, over the powerful influence of the Lady Loon. A male jaguar prowled the damp forest ground while the other made her way around."

Peony spins in a circle, "Hungry and thirsty they both came to waterfalls with thick overgrown trees and vine covered rock walls. To drink water pure and pristine in the rainforest's crystal-clear stream. Jade's eyes a dark emerald green hue, Rosa's eyes are the color of golden bamboo. They glance at each other in a polite gaze, while fog encloses the rainforest in a blanket of misty haze. The sunrise on the horizon with rays across the sky, as the two giant jaguars go walking by. The sound of falling water breaks the silence of the woodland tomb, as the Wood Witch steps out of her Banyan home with a long-handled broom. She wears a dress of bark and moss with wild auburn hair of root and rust. She waves around the bristle broom that sparkles like diamond dust. She encircles around the jaguar lady who enters into a trancelike dream. Awakening to see her reflection in the calm, clear running stream; to her amazement she has been changed into a beautiful, bejeweled Queen. Then around the other jaguar she spun a circle there, waving her broom high up in the air, while they stood standing together in a pair. In a shower of shimmer, he became a warrior with long brown braided hair."

Peony poses in perfect posture as she continues to sing, "He wore a hide of tan leather, she wore sheer golden lace, he wore a beaded head feather, a jeweled snake framed her face. Transformed to jaguars at dusk, then back into humans by dawn. Living inside a Banyan Tree on the banks of Lake Black Swan. Sunrise to sunset they gathered huckleberries to eat, blueberries, blackberries and strawberries so sweet. Waxing and waning lunar cycles of time went by, big black cats sleeping in a Banyan bedroom where they lie. Hunting brigades with torches and blades march by every full moon. The forest felines sleep in secret to the Night Jasmines' sweet perfume. Hidden in the canopy of the Banyans' branch embrace, lay the two lost lovers in a perfect private place. Many a man come looking for them in the jungle to take them back. The only scene they ever saw were two jaguars big and black. Disappearing into the shadows when they hear the hunters come, eating in their food forest of pear, peach and plum. Their Companionship gives them comfort in this dank, dark land.

With its groves of Banyan trees, a liquid lake and fine black sand. In an extraordinary sanctuary under a lush canopy of trees, lay these two jungle jaguars in soft moss and evening breeze. Their branch house hidden by an abundance of thriving leaves, hiding their fruit and nut supply from the eyes of wild life thieves. Having evening dreams, under starlight beams with their lantern lamp a Crescent Moon, sleeping soundly serenaded by the lovely Lady Loon."

Peony spins around again in a circle with her wings expanded like two fluffy feather fans. Dancing gracefully across the stage covering herself with her wings before backing out through the cobweb curtains. The entire audience claps and cheers loudly calling out, "Miracle!" "Miracle!"

CHAPTER 6

Spanish Peacock

A light and dark gray raccoon tilts back his broad brimmed hat. Smiling at the audience, he begins to play an intense tempo on a carved acoustic guitar. A trio of squirrels join in with the raccoon harmonizing on their own guitars. Clicking castanets can be heard in the background as a beautiful blue and green peacock enters into the lit up mushroom circle.

The proud peacock begins a flamenco dance and starts to sing, "I have come to perform for you, I'm Lazuli Balsam of Peru! Through the wilderness over grassy hills of Bluebells, Jonquils and Daffodils. A caravan of gypsy wagons painted in brightly colored hue, drawn by many horses to a valley encampment new. With their coats of coal and coats of cream, horses and goats grazed in fields of green. Inside a painted vardo wagon was a gypsy lady, Sahara Wildfire Dawn, with her bother Romi, whom she doted on. On her eighteenth birthday she made a Lilac Lavender lotion, on her nineteenth, longing a soulmate, she made a Desert Rose love potion. She took out a Rosette crystal from a box made of cedar wood, to place it on a red orange table where all her ingredients stood. She grasped her copper caldron and brought it to the fire pit. Then heated up honey, herbs and water she mixed and matched mead with it. Sahara placed three pinches of Damiana into the teakettle, stirring Rose Hips, Cinnamon, Nutmeg and Nettle.

Sahara tasted it with a shiny spoon as she began to chant to a Strawberry Moon, *'I am a single girl calling with two hearts of quartz stone rose, that under the stars and sunlight grows. Three silver spoons of honey gold, awaken the power of the old. Three spoon sips of brandy wine, you are divine, you shall be mine, your heart shall be my valentine. From now until eternity, you have my heart so shall it be.'*

One day Sahara rode into town in her long, red, ruffled lace gown. Accompanied by Romi playing a mandolin, while his friend Bo fiddles a violin.

The people all stopped to watch as a coin or two is tossed into a leather case of Celtic knots embossed. A Bohemian boy past by and sees Sahara dancing there, he watches her in the center of the town square. Sahara looks into his brown eyes and her heart skips a beat; she knew he was the man to sweep her of her feet. When she finished, he came to greet her, to tell her his name was Jack, he is tall, lean and strong with long hair, thick and black.

Sahara asks, *'Would you like your fortune told in exchange for only one coin of gold? I can read with cards, coins, Rune stones, gaze into a crystal ball or even roll the bones! I am herbalist and have real remedies where I tincture many flowers, roots and trees. I have rabbits, chickens, goats and pet raccoons. I also own a copper cauldron, fire pit and silver spoons.'*

Jack is quite intrigued, so he asks, *'Yet, can you cook?'*

Sahara nods with a smile and gives him a wide-eyed look then replies, *'I have so many recipes I could write a book!'*

Lazuli dances over to Lady Camellia and Lord Obsidian, turning in a circle shaking large peacock plumage while singing, *"Jack tells her 'There is a wailing woman who sobs a heavy moan, while banging on my door at midnight at my home. I looked out the window but no one is ever there, though she continues to bang on the walls everywhere.'*

Sahara replies, 'It sounds like a Banshee or an Unseelie Selkie, it's a ill omen of what will come to be. I will make you an amulet with Mandrake, Wolfsbane and a black Tourmaline stone, wear it on a chain to protect you when she comes again to your home. Do not open the door to this dangerous and disturbing ghost, as she is looking for somebody that she can have to host.'

Sahara takes Jack to her vardo wagon with a sign that read Taboo, inside was more than enough room for the two. A shining sunset takes on a glorious hue as she brings out her crystal ball, knowing what to do.

She looks into the ominous orb and sees a vision in her sight of the wispy wailing woman floating in the fields at night. Sahara says, *'It seems she was unhappy in life and that there was once foul play, before she passed into the realms of the Netherworld away. Tilling the soil, weeding broken bones where your house does stand, I'm watching the woman wraith haunting you there upon that land.'*

Jack agrees, *'Yes, I know, I dug up bones in my corn crop. What do I have to do now to get this curse to stop?'*

Sahara hands him a Mojo bag shaking her head, *'Unfortunately, Jack this is your fault. Here, take this sage stick, a seashell and some salt. You chose coin over conscious, so now you pay a different price, you must sprinkle this salt clockwise around your house for three nights thrice. Keep this Mojo Bag on your neck tightly bound, while you burn the Sage in your house and sprinkle it on the ground. Salt and smoke in every room corner, chanting a HU vowel sound. When you see the Bluebird of Happiness, you'll know Pandora's Box has closed. To trap this ghastly ghoul outside so her frightening you will be opposed.'*

Lazuli dances around the fairy ring then spins around in the center spotlight to finish the song singing, "Throughout the cycle of one year until it ends, Jack and Sahara became very close friends. The wailing woman left to rest in peace and her banging on his doors and walls did finally cease. Then once upon a Midsummers Day, Jack gives Sahara a golden ring and asks, *'Will you stay with me and be my wife? I really need more luck in my life.'*

Sahara laughs and replies, *'Yes, I will, then we'll both be free of strife.'*

They are married inside the square in the center of town. Her brother plays a fiddle when she enters in her white lace, ruffled gown. They say their vows in a loving embrace as he caresses her hair, kissing her pretty face. There is a feast in the encampment with bonfires lit, pots and pans with copper kettles cooking over the fire pit.

Everyone talking with friends and family, feasting on food and mead. A band makes merry music for their union to succeed. Jack carries her over the threshold of his humble home, of the door, where there before, a wailing woman did roam."

Lazuli shakes to open the many tail feathers into one feather fan while turning in a slow circle for everyone to see before bowing and exiting offstage.

The guests all cheer and applaud, "Miracle!"

The dark shadow returns to cross over Lazuli as a giant bat follows to swoop straight down standing right in front of the panicking peacock. The grotesque looking bat smiles revealing his sharp pointy teeth. He tips his hat and bows at the flabbergasted fowl. Lazuli is visibly shaken, seeing the big bad bat is quite intimidating.

"Let me introduce myself, my name is Sangue Diavolo, I am the owner of the Lucky Ducky Club you know. I'm looking for a singer such as yourself to star in my show, so why don't you come with me? I will show you the way to go."

Lazuli replies, "Why Mr. Diavolo you're very charming, even if your appearance is really quite alarming."

Diavolo winks one eye, "Come with me now my pet and I will show you a night you shall never forget."

"It's a tempting offer you propose Mr. Bat, but I'm afraid my friends would wonder where I was at." Lazuli steps backwards trying not to trip.

Diavolo steps forward closer to the pretty peacock. "It won't take long, the club is not far from here, come now you can trust me my dear."

"I don't think tonight will be a good time to go, I have to meet with a friend to watch the moon bow."

Lazuli continues to step backwards as the brown hairy bat steps forward, "Come with me, I will sweep you off your feet, you are such a beautiful bird and I bet you taste so sweet!"

Diavolo grabs Lazuli quickly holding the peacock plumage in his skinny arms while wrapping his large wings snugly around his victim like a spider to a fly.

Diavolo states, "Under this dark mysterious night, I shall want to take a bite!" He opens his mouth placing it against Lazuli's neck.

Lazuli bites Diavolo hard on his nose; the bat grabs his face with both hands freeing the peacock from his grasp. Diavolo looks up and Lazuli slaps him across the face screaming, "You want to try to bite me, then I will bite you back, you are just a vicious villain and you deserve a good smack!"

Diavolos' eyes widen as his face changes into one of shock, pointing at the puffed-up peacock shouting, "No wonder you are stronger than I am, YOU'RE NOT A LADYBIRD AT ALL, YOU ARE A BIRD GENT MAN!"

Lazuli replies sarcastically, "In the feathers to be sure, you looking for a ladybird to lure? Now I'm going to go warn all the others, how you deserve to be bit! Your behavior is outrageous and we will not allow it!"

Lazuli proceeds to run quickly away into the darkness while Diavolo shouts behind him angerly, "I will have my revenge on you for your judgment you lack! YOU CRAZY PEACOCK! YOU BETTER WATCH YOUR BACK!"

Diavolo starts to leave as he sees a shadow moving quickly in the distance coming his way. He runs quickly behind a giant fern to hide. Peeking out he sees a fluffy, feminine flamingo making her way out into the center of the fairy ring. Diavolo drools as she passes by him however, she doesn't see him hidden in the darkness. The big, bad bat stares directly at her face then down at her long legs.

30

CHAPTER 7

French Flamingo

A vibrant, pink flamingo is walking on point gracefully on the tips of her toes like a ballerina fanning her fluffy feathers. A classical sonata begins to resonate by a raccoon playing piano with many chipmunks puffing on horns and brass instruments. Rabbits blow on horns and clarinets and a single skunk wearing a trench coat and plays a saxophone. Meadow mice on woodwinds perform with perfect pitch as Bumble Bees buzz behind her beating on bongos. The French flamingo sings out to the audience, "I am Fifi LeFleur alive to allure, to tell you the secret language of flowers; from the thorns on the briers, to the blossoms on the bowers."

Fifi dances over while spinning around on her toes with her soft feathered wings outstretched. She stands before Lady Camellia and Lord Obsidian singing out softly, "Say you will bring me a rose for my hair, a token to convey your love, say you will stay with me one lifetime to share our love as free as a dove. We can have long talks on the vine and be lovebirds in no time! Bring me a flower of how you feel about me, a Canterbury Bell to show consistency. Will it be a Sweet Pea, a message that our love is meant to be? Will you bring a Chrysanthemum that your love is no longer or an intoxicating Poppy that our love is growing stronger? How about a Sweet William a show of gallantry or a Lady Slipper of my beauty rarity? An offering of Queen Anne's Lace to say I have a pretty face? Will it be a Larkspur, Lobelia, Lily or Foxglove? What flower will you bring me to express to me your love? How about a Morning Glory, Snap Dragon or Nutmeg spice, to tell me I'm intelligent, honest and nice? A Tiger Lily to say I'm silly or a Violet to say I'm coy or how about a simple Daisy to say I bring you joy? If you find a four-leaf Clover to tell me I am lucky you are mine, I will be overjoyed by that special sign!"

Fifi twirls around the ring with her feather fans high above her, "Mistletoe placed above my head, shows me that chivalry is not dead. A Marigold for a faith most gallant or a Bachelors Button for hope that is valiant. Purple Heather for all my wishes to come true or faithfulness with a violet blue. A simple Sunflower for pleasant memories spent or a White Gardenia a secret romance with a handsome gent. A Tulip, declaration of your love for me or a Crocus would make me very happy. A Tuberose is a symbol of purity of mind. A bending Brier twig, true love is hard to find. A Zinnia you mourn my absence, so you want to clear the air, or a poisonous Oleander to tell me to beware. Show me how you feel for me with the secret language of flowers. Is it thorns on the briers, or blossoms on the bowers? When you're ripe, you're rotten, when you're green you're growing. Which of these fragrant flowers will you be showing? Or how about the rare Lotus Blue, to tell me you want marry me and want to say I do? I wait in vain, in pouring rain, to get a flower from you! I hope you will find to change your mind and dream of love under October skies, when lovebirds begin to open their eyes. Dancing together to a waltz orchestra, that would be most jeno se qua, so hand me a ring, then I shall sing, oh sir oooh la la!"

Fifi kicks the air while pointing her toes twirling around while smiling, "Do you suppose you could bring me a rose as a message you still love me? This is what I really want from you, you see. Into this empty room I wish you would strut, I don't need anyone else but, say you will bring me one rose for my hair, a symbol to wear of your love, say you will come to me, that you really care, an offering of peace from a dove. I want you to remember when my petals wilt and dies, like the rose you shall give to me with passion in your eyes. A baby bud to show how you really feel about me, that I still haunt your memory. A single red rose to show your passion, a bright yellow rose, well friendships always in fashion. A pink one for true love, orange for creativity, a red-orange rose to symbol prosperity. The white rose of course represents purity. Will you surprise me with one so rare, a purple color one to adorn in my hair? This is the message of this royal rose you see, that you want to share your life with me.

Don't bring me Myrtle to symbolize despair or a Daffodil of unrequited love we don't share. Bring me the gift of a perfect rose in any color hue, show me your love for me is pure and true. So, come what may, I shall wait here each day, for a flower from my beloved, that's you!"

Fifi spins around in a circle with her pink wings out stretched then turns to pose with her wings coming together to form a heart. She curtsies before exiting the spotlight the out through the cobweb curtains.

There are roars of cheers, clapping wildly and repeated calls from the various attendees of "Miracle"!

Diavolo dusts himself off as he steps out from his hiding place to go after Fifi. A solid black raven prepares to perform next, Diavolo is not aware of the bird in the darkness and he begins to talk to himself out loud while folding his hands together. The raven pauses his movement to listen.

"Well, my fascinating Flamingo with your fluffy feathers of pretty pink, you give me an idea, you inspire me to think. A most scrumptious sight that I have ever seen, I ask you, all my life Miss Fifi, where you have been? Even though I'm as blind as a bat, I'm so full of surprises, for I can still make out colors, shapes and sizes. I shall have to take her when no one else shall see, to the other side of Phantom Island to the ancient cemetery. We will tiptoe through the tombstones into the abandoned church that's near here. A crumbling castle with a withering red rose stained glass mirror. Then no one will know where she is at, since I am a Vampire Bat, I plan to become quite fat!"

His black eyes shine with renewed excitement as he laughs wickedly dancing around in the damp dirt. Diavolo Confidently adjusts his tie and vest as a final fix before flying out of the thick forest. He twists and twirls upward while watching and waiting for Fifi below.

CHAPTER 8

African Raven

Storm clouds begin to gather together creating a thick
foreboding fog. Thunder booms and flashes of lightning
strike down from the dismal sky as the tenor raven slowly
sings, "I am so sad to hear this news, thinking about it
only gives me the blues. I must warn the others, the plots
and plans of this Vampire Bat! We must search high and low
to find where he is hiding at! Oh, heavenly Nightingale
wherever you are, please hear this prayer under the morning
star, that you may protect Fifi is my only lament and stop
this bat from finding her wherever she went. The legend of
the Nightingale in all her silver glory was created from a
myth passed down in years of story. So, I sing this song
for you Nightingale for wherever you are at, to protect our
Miss LaFluer from the claws of this Vampire Bat."

The raven walks front and center in the middle of the
spotlight. He stands still in front of Camellia and
Obsidian. A pair of gray wolves start to play; one on piano
and the other strumming a bass guitar. A black bear strums
a haunting hymn on a cello.

The raven Begins to croon, "I am Onyx, a raven of
poetry, Rhythm and Blues, now I shall sing a sad song and
share with you some news- You, all I ever wanted was you,
trying to do the best I can do. Why do I always try so
hard? It never gets me far, doesn't matter I only long for
you. Pain that you bring, you're never realizing what
you're doing to me, love is such a crazy game, all results
the same. Can we solve it? Will we ever be? I can see it
in your eyes, we could bring the magic alive, forever and
never hide only you and I."

Thunder crackles loudly as lightning flashes out in
all directions from the low floating clouds. Onyx watches
the sky and starts to sing, "I wanted to be there for you,
after all we been through, you left me when I needed you
most, your memory is just a faceless ghost. I cannot see or
talk to you, it's like your death and funeral too.

36

     Your memory keeps haunting me, I thought our love was
meant to be. My heart beats only for you, for a love pure
and true that I pined away all of the day and all of the
lonely night too. For once I was in love and happy, now I
am sad and blue. My smile has faded away, like the sun's
final day, I shed tears like drops of dew. My heart aches
for you as you have gone from my sight, so now I long all
the day, full of dismay far off into the night. My soul
feels so strong for my beloved has gone; the darkness has
taken over the light. You, all I ever cared about is you,
thinking about us only makes me blue. You made this choice
to give, I have my life to live, it's over now, our
precious love is through. I can see it in your eyes we can
keep the magic alive, forever and never, hold only you and
I."
     Onyx walks around in a drizzling fog before the dark
clouds above begin to cry rain. Raven sings sadly, "Now,
I'm finding the strength to be strong, as you have been
gone away so long. I cannot imagine this would be my fate,
to sit, wonder and contemplate, that it's just another case
of hurry up and wait. They say the eyes are the windows to
the soul, but I feel I've lost all control, this emptiness
inside is something I can't hide. My love I cannot fake it
and the waiting I cannot take it. I reminisce of our
rendezvous with us kissing, it's only you I'm missing. Even
though you had to go, I don't want anyone else so- With
this feeling so intense, I just sit here on the fence. I
must learn self-mastery, for it is a fine art, or will I
just be here in fear, my dear, with my broken heart?"

     Lightning streaks down from the sky brightening up his
silhouette afterwards thunder crackles loudly. Onyx
continues to croon, "I don't understand where we went wrong
or why we just can't get along? They say what doesn't kill
you only makes you stronger however I cannot wait here any
longer. I say this sincerely with a tear in my eye. How can
you leave me without saying goodbye? Now it is clear, I
know there was a reason for all those tears, you gave me
something to fear, but it's you who loses my dear, I'll
pick up the pieces now and get my flight in gear. I can see
it in your eyes we could bring our magic alive, forever and
never, has forgotten you and I."

CHAPTER 9

Magnolia and Merlot

Two black and white magpies are eating red plums in a distant tree when they see flashes of lightning through the forest. Milton Merlot is a love-sick butler who wears a tuxedo and a black derby hat. His partner Magnolia Jasmine Snow is dressed in a fancy, frilly black and white maid's attire. Startled but curious they fly up and over the fruit trees to get a closer look. That's when they both hear the soulful raven crooning. Gliding down to get a better look they approach cautiously, perching for a better view in a nearby Evergreen tree they investigate the activities inside the fairy ring.

Merlot grabs Magnolias' wing as they slow dance on the pine wood branch to the raven's woeful lyrics. Onyx continues to sing his lucid lullaby as the magpies look at each other seductively. Merlot puts his wing out for her smirking at the thought of attending the party below and dancing with her in his wings despite the thunder, lightning and pouring rain.

"Excuse me my fine feathered lady, it would be such a charming delight, if you would come walk and talk with me this fine day before late tonight. You are such a gorgeous girl, I can only grin. Or perhaps would you rather go dancing? I could give you a whirl, a twirl and a spin."

"Why thank you kind sir, I'm flattered, I'm sure; it will be such a pleasant surprise, for me to come walk and talk with you this fine day, under dark gloomy skies. You're such a refined classy gentleman, as handsome as so you are wise." Magnolia rolls her eyes and nods her head.

"Thank you, Miss Magnolia my beautiful black-eyed crow, let's dance together before you have to go, back to The Lucky Ducky Club where life is always the same. Now let's take a stroll, past the grassy knoll, down to Henny Penny Lane."

Diavolo hears the magpies talking in the distance. He flies in the direction of the two confident voices. Suddenly swooping down from out of the foggy shadows to stand next to them. Diavolo tips his hat smiling deviously in their direction, "Good evening madpies, wait, just a minute before you go, I need to talk to both of you, it's most urgent you know!"

Magnolia puts her wings on her hips, "Why Mr. Diavolo it's my day off today, so *get* out of our way! I will be back tomorrow. I'm off to dance with Mr. Merlot, for I only have time left to borrow!"

"No, no," Diavolo says desperately, "I'm here to make you a deal, where you'll never miss a meal! A generous offer to give, the best treehouse to live! But first, I must get the eagle and owl out of the way, after all they are birds of prey. We must plot a plan to create bait, we can all capture the firebird and not have to wait. We must do it *now* before it's too late!"

Merlot complains, "Just any attempt won't work as her magic would strike us dead!"

Diavolo looks at him scolding, "While Ember's asleep place her in a cage of steel and lead, this is the only way to make sure she's dead! She must be in it for twenty-four hours before the metal completely destroys her powers! Then after three days she will lose all her fire feather, turning them to ash destroying her all together!"

Merlot asks grimly, "What will we earn in return?"

"It's their life force I wish to drink. How can we do it? Give me a chance to think. Once we get Sage, Rune and Ember out of the way I can take one bird every day, until each bird has gone away. Then the food forest will belong to both of you, no competition to eat, the land you'll own for only you two. So, this is my offer in a nutshell, when you help me capture all the birds of paradise you two will have the best place to dwell!"

Magnolia flutters her eyelashes at him smiling, "That is a grand idea Mr. Bat but not to be rude- How do you plan to leave us all the food? You ought to leave the plan up to Mr. Merlot and I to make all the birds comply."

Diavolo replies, "For indeed its greed, which feeds my need, I *insist* upon the help from the two of you to succeed! For I've already tipped my hand as well as my hat, the birds now know I'm out for blood because I'm a Vampire Bat!" The big, bad bat laughs wickedly while walking in circles around the couple.

Merlot points his right wing up smiling smugly, "It's like pawns in a game of chess, making our next move is our only guess. We need to put our heads together to first get rid of Sage, Rune and Ember. We will think of a way and we must do it today!"

Magnolia steps forward toward the Vampire Bat stating, "Sage guards Ember with his sharp eagle eye, her guardian protector perched on his mountain high. He watches the birds by day from the tip top of Pyramid Peak because it's Ember's wisdom in which they all seek. While he sleeps at night, it's Rune who watches over them with his far-seeing vision in Pansflorawood Glen."

Diavolo scratches the back of his head and whispers, "We must find a way, let's say- Using our natural born skills, we setup a scene that has a theme to break their wills. Create an illusion of confusion, something that thrills!"

Magnolia winks one eye, "You know I'm the best deceiver, I can make even the most skeptical a believer. I can tell a bigger and bigger lie over and over until they never question why."

Merlot says sternly, "I will be like a thief in the night robbing you blind, then I will take off in flight. I can pick the lock to any safe guarded treasure. Why to help you Mister Diavolo sir it will be my pleasure."

Merlot reaches out his wing to shake Diavolos' claw
like hand while shrugging his shoulders in excitement.
Diavolo puts his sharp claws around the two magpies with a
warning tone in his voice, "Magnolia, my pretty ladybird I
do contend, Milton, a bird of your word, my closest trusted
friend; we'll put our plan together and with the help of
both of you, it will give me something I can really sink my
teeth into. All our evil genius, we have in our brains, I
know by persistence, reluctance, resistance, we'll get our
ill-gotten gains."

Magnolia looks at both of them with her big, black,
devious eyes shifting back and forth hissing, "I want to
stomp and crush on any ladybirds dream, planting a seed of
destruction, where things are *not* what they seem. I *know we
three* make a great team!"

Merlot turns to Diavolo asking, "How will you get them
to trust you? It won't be *that* easy to do. You have to
create something interesting- Wait, I have an idea coming
through. We will fashion with our imagination, an illusion
of confusion. A night of entertainment served with
delicious delights! Dazzling up the darkness in orange and
purple lights! We'll distract them with an Autumn Festival
Ball! We'll have food, fun and drink to give them all, on a
Feast O' Full of Fall!"

Diavolo spins around happily with his wings
outstretched throwing his hat high up into the air then
catching it laughing, "YES! it's a perfect plan to plot a
play, to confuse the birds thus getting the eagle, owl and
phoenix out of the way! What you tell them this evening
wearing a dismal disguise, when all the birds come together
to sleep under starlit skies. Tell them before they go to
sleep tonight in Pansflorawood Glen, details all about this
ball of how, where, why and when!"

Magnolia quickly manifests a flower crown placing it
on top of her head she cackles, "Tempting the ladybirds for
one to be crowned the Green Queen, a competition between
every flying female where they all dance, prance and sing.
Trust me, those dumb dames won't suspect a thing.

We tell them we're throwing a sensational seasonal masquerade ball every Winter, Spring, Summer and Fall!"

Diavolo dances around the mischievous magpies waving his bat cape wings up in the air singing excitedly, "All come one, one come all, to the Autumn Pumpkin Ball! Come bee, come bug, come bird, come bat, come to the ball from wherever you're at! We'll feast during the day, then dance night away! Underneath a moss-covered mound, underground, where when they scream there won't be a sound! We'll hold it three moons from now at the violet twilight, on this coming Equinox known as All Hallows Eve night! By the stream at the edge of the forest, between the two hills that match, is a boundless and bountiful overgrown pumpkin patch! It's the perfect place to hold a masquerade ball where we will be in costume so they won't recognize us at all! We'll be incognito in all the bird's sight, on the eerie evening known as the witch's night!"

Magnolia walks over, holding her wings out in front of her speaking loudly, "Under the spell of a big, bright blue moon there once born a bud of Belladonna Bloom. It is a bramble bush with burgundy blossoms known as the Nightmare Nightshade. We can make a toxic drink from it for the masquerade. Its flowers are born from the blackest of berry, growing plentiful in the old cemetery. To fetch it on a new moon eve will be very scary. We must go over hill, over dale, under fern frond canopy veils to find it under a Deadwood Tree. We leave on this Waxing Moon tonight so we can all three see. We shall make a Belladonna Brew from the Nightmare Nightshade, a potent, poison potion, from the berry of it's made. The birds shall fall into a deep sound sleep, then the food forest will be ours to keep! I need every part of the plant root, berry and flower, for no bird can resist its power." She uses her wings to mimic a full flower opening.

"Let's go now to find this Nightmare Nightshade so all the birds will take a dirt nap from the poison potion that we've made! We must mix it with another liquid to disguise the flavor, like the Cherry Berry Vine Wine that all the birds favor. We must go collect the Cherry Vine for we are running out of time! To disguise our Belladonna Brew to lead them all astray, now follow me my fine feathered friends, I know the way!" Merlot waves his wings about before pointing in the direction they all should follow.

Magnolia, Merlot and Diavolo caw and cackle wickedly as one by one they fly off into the thick woodland, disappearing into the surrounding pitch blackness.

CHAPTER 10

Norse Owl

Free floating clouds are turning all colors of the rainbow as a large, muscular Snowy Owl steps slowly into the center of the fairy ring. He makes his way into the spotlight then stops to turn his head in every direction. All the woodland animals play their instruments together into a synchronous symphony. The Norse owl bows to Lady Camellia and Lord Obsidian while wearing a silver helmet decorated with two white wings on each side. He looks out at the audience again as the images reflect of his story in the foggy mist while transforming into a cloud castle.

In his deep booming Baritone voice, he starts to sing, "Yoo-hoo! How do you do? I'm a Snowy Owl, call me Rune, guardian of the birds, I fly in the eve by the moon. Once there was a Galaxy called The Eye in the Sky, a shining, sparkling, spiral where cloud castles go floating by. Here the Valkyrie Goddesses on their Pegasus fly, capturing Warriors in battles that die, in puddles of blood on Earth where they lie. One such Valkyrie named Aura Wren, was off one day to gather warriors again. She secretly wished for a man of her own to keep, as she flew over valleys and mountains so steep. One day she landed in a battlefield of red, filled with the corpses of the men who were dead. Aura collected their souls inside a crystal ball, to take them to King Odin at Valhalla Hall."

Rune dances very slowly around the circle stopping every now and then to pose and turn his head while using his wings to help tell his sing-song story, "One of the men was handsome, pale and cold in death, slain by a sword that stole his last breath. Aura claimed his soul into an amulet, for without him she could not part. She wore it as a necklace, his immortal spirit kept near and dear to her heart. Aura placed her hand into his long hair dark and brown, with his frazzled face turned into a twisted, tangled frown. Flying his frozen body to her cloud castle with the coming of the dawn, she placed him on a silky bed, the lifeless man of muscle, brain and brawn. The misty fog

44

swirled around Aura, a dark disturbing gray as the sunset sank away into another dusky day. Other Valkyries came to find her ordered by wise King Odin, to meet on Moonshine Mountain to set a time, what day, where and when. Aura had no choice, under Odin's voice, to take the corpse to the Green Ash tree, there the Earth shall open up to swallow him into eternity."

Rune walks slowly in front of the Flora Fae and Fauna Wood court continuing to sing, "With a tear in her eye she began to cry, wondering what this man was like when he was alive. Aura, was willing to save his soul for his battle crime, she knew he was to be sent to the Underworld, cursed until the end of time. Aura vowed to protect him and told Odin in the warrior's defense, all of the good deeds he did while he was alive in her voice most intense.

She asked King Odin, 'Can I take him into my sacred space?' He nodded, agreed and gently grabbed her face.

'King Odin, can I bring him back from the dead?' King Odin smiled, 'Of course my child,' then softly kissed her forehead.

Rune quickly turns around to walk into the spotlight singing, "With the talisman around her neck and the warrior an empty shell, she took him in secret with her, not a soul did she tell. Winged Pegasus flies them over a roaring sea, to spare his spirit she quickly had to flee. Above the towering mountains to find the old wishing well, to use its healing waters to consecrate her spell. She chanted ancient incantations she once memorized, envisioning him awakening, looking at her with open eyes. Aura drew from the Fountain of Life, as the ritual she did follow, to pour the healing waters into his mouth for him to swallow. Chanting for him to be reborn again with a life of flesh, blood and bone, she made him drink the fountains water where he woke to moan and groan. His eyes opened from his death sleep, Aura thanked the Gods for granting her wish of a man to love and keep. She put the Alexandrite Amulet back into her purse and wondered if the consequence of her actions would be a blessing or a curse.

Once upon her Pegasus into the heavens they flew, to be welcomed home with mead and feast her handsome husband new. There was a celebration at Valhalla Hall with all ancestors at the palace. Filled with music melodies while feasting with honey wine in a silver chalice. Under radiant rainbow rays of Aurora Borealis glowing, facing each other, Aura in her green gown freely flowing. Snow White Gardenias adorning her carrot ginger hair. Having a handsome husband holding her with tender loving care. A smile returns upon his face as they kiss and hug in a long embrace. They swore to each other to be the best that they can, she is his heart and soul and he was her eternal, immortal man."

Rune turns his head on a swivel as he marches out of the fairy ring. The audience claps and cheers, "Miracle!"

Just off stage attending to some last-minute preening is an albino albatross waiting for his cue. Sage catches up to Rune backstage as he is taking off his helmet in front of a broken mirror. Rune sees Sage in the mirrors reflection behind him and turns his head to face him.

Sage asks laughingly, "Are you ready for sleep now my good friend? I'm surprised to see you up and around."

Rune replies in his deep voice, "Yes, I was up late last night since I found a new hunting ground."

Just then Lazuli appears from behind Rune and Sage frantically flailing feathers, "Here you are my fine feathered friends, it seems the drama around here just never ends! I have some news for both of you, this just happened to me I tell you it is true! There is a Vampire Bat on the loose, looking for a ladybird to cook her goose! That same bat tried to take a bite out of me, draining all my life force energy! Soon he should be found, to be scorned and scattered, torn and tattered, so he'll never come back around!"

Sage turns to Rune sounding concerned, "I will go find Ember to warn her of this Vampire Bat."

Lazuli crosses his wings, "He wears a striped suit, spats for shoes and has a *stupid* looking hat!"

Rune puts his wing to his forehead turning his head all the way around looking for any sign of trouble replying, "I shall keep my Hawk eyes out for him tonight, since it is the night time when he'll try to take a bite."

Sage hurries and flies off to find and warn Ember. Flapping his wings as fast as he can into the direction of the distant steaming volcano.

CHAPTER 11

Scottish Albatross

Being careful not to step on any of the smaller guests around him Alabaster albatross approaches the fairy ring. A sea turtle plays on a set of bagpipes as seagulls laugh to the beat and play flutes and fiddles. Alabasters' feathers are light purple, he pats them down on his chest before adjusting his plaid cap and checkered kilt.

Alabaster takes a pose before boasting out loudly, "Out in the distance of a forbidden sea an old schooner ship went sailing free. On board this ship were a captain and crew of pirates who sailed the ocean blue. All were brutally handsome young men, a lust for desire with passion within. A want for adventure, a need for gold; for each of these pirates the brave and the bold. Only one held a longing for a love that was true, the captain, who sailed the ocean blue. A desire so deep from the depths of his heart, depths like the ocean, he never would part. One day he landed in a turquoise lagoon, with a coral castle lit up by the light of the moon. The gilded ship landed upon a sandy shore before the men marched up to the structure with a Scallop, seashell door. They all separated to have a look around, while the captain searched alone inside the courtyard ground."

Alabaster shuffles his feet around performing a folk style clog dance as he moves closer to Lady Camellia and Lord Obsidian. The Albatross opens his giant wings up over his head still singing, "Standing high on a balcony was a lovely lass is whom he found, she moved in a long, flowing, glittering gown. Her lengthy white hair in the wind was wildly blowing, as she stood still like a sensuous spirit illuminating and glowing. In the flora and fauna with all the shades of green was like a scene that you would see only in a dream. The lovely lady came down to meet him with her body floating free; her eyes were the color of the foam of the sea. When their eyes met, they could not look away, for each of them wanted the other to stay. In an uncontrollable long embrace, they touched and caressed each other's face.

The yearning of love that each of them missed was finally fulfilled when both of them kissed. Bewitched that first moment he looked into her eyes, he could not let her go to say their goodbyes.

He says, *'I shall take you with me and you will be my bride.'*

'Oh no, I'm sorry sir,' she softly replied, *'I shall be taken by the tide.'*

He carried her off to the ship schooner, this maiden fair, in the long glowing gown with the long flowing hair. Now back at the boat, in the salty air, into his chambers he took her there then placed her upon an antique chair. He locked her inside his parlor room where she drew a bath with candles and a bottle of Rose perfume. She undressed to step into the bath water pool to sit in the fragrance of calming cool. As soon as she soaked, she shapeshifted a tail, with sparkling fin and opalescent scale. The mermaiden called out the captain's name, *'James McCoy.'* Haunted whispers down the corridor until he finally came. He followed her siren song that finally sealed his fate as he made his way to find her and could hardly wait. He took his chance to take her, not knowing he would invite a curse of the *Rime of the Ancient Mariner*. When he walked into the room, one word she finally spoke, it was the word *'husband'* with the curse it did invoke. Before he could blink, she quickly grabbed his hand; they dove through the open window from where the man did stand. Falling down into a dark abyss, the mermaid and mariner flew, into the deep cold waters, through the depths of the ocean blue. Here she will capture his soul forever, for he was her rare buried treasure. Even as her prisoner, his soul was set free, floating along, singing a song, into the depths of the deep blue sea. To this day lost passing ships, hear her siren song on a waning moon and evening eclipse.

The mermaiden sings a haunting tune falling from her full lips, *'Looking across a vast rolling ocean, blue and deep with waves of emotion, listening to nature's perfect tune, while I wait in time for a changing moon.'*

49

The curse changed the captain's legs into a triton's tail, with a pale iridescent scale and a fish fin that slowly grew, to swim with his mermaiden through the depths of the ocean blue."

Alabaster takes a bow at the applause by the fading spotlight before turning to exit the outside of the fairy ring. The audience of creatures and critters clap and cheer while calling out, "Miracle!"

CHAPTER 12

Belladonna Brew

Magnolia slowly holds up the crimson-colored blossom with her right wing showing it to Merlot, "Under the waning crescent moon, we found the blackberry bunch in bloom- So now here's what we're going to do, mix it in with the Cherry Berry Vine Wine to make Belladonna Brew."

Merlot straightens his bow tie chuckling, "We must tell the birds today of the ball in the overgrown pumpkin patch, we'll make sure Ember attends, for it's *her* we really want to catch."

Diavolo folds his wings over his chest angrily, "*Well I* certainly cannot do it they know me and my name, my reputation as the big, bad bat with no shame in my game. I tried to capture Ember once before, trying to gain her trust, but in return she tried to turn me into a blaze of fire dust!"

Magnolia steps closer towards Diavolo swaying her hips speaking convincingly, "Since I'm the perfect one to spy, as your own private eye, I can convince the birds of any lie. First, we give Ember the Belladonna Brew to drink, when she fades off to sleep, she won't be able to think. We will put her in a place where no bird will ever find her, a place she *cannot* escape to permanently bind her."

Merlot scowls raising his eyebrows as his eyes widen, "Precisely Princess, the three of us will crawl and creep while All the Birds of Paradise fade off into a deep sleep. Then the food forest will be ours to keep! We must capture Ember by midnight, when the tick tock of the clock will chime, then we will fly back to put her into the theater of time. First, we take Sage, Onyx and Rune far up Mariner's Cape blocking the caves entrance so they cannot escape! Next will be Lazuli and Peony, we can place in the old Oak tree, piling rocks all around them, so that they cannot break free!"

Diavolo narrows his eyes squinting while rubbing his wings together, "With the owl and eagle out of the way, Miss Fifi Lafleur will be easy prey. Ember must be the first to go, since she's the only one with magical powers you know. Peony and Lazuli will be easy too, with this flower power of Belladonna Brew! Most importantly when you lock them away see that they *still* have their heartbeat, they are no good to me dead! They must be alive to eat!"

Magnolia shows the Belladonna bloom to the Vampire Bat before laughing loudly, "We have the perfect place to plot and plan a play, let's go soon to invite all the birds to get them to come and stay. I know they are all still performing in the fairy ring waiting to take their bow, let's go inform them of the Masquerade Ball, let's get this show on the road- Now!"

Diavolo hides his face in his batwing cape only revealing his glowing beady eyes, "This is my time of the evening when I am a predator for prey! After all I am a Vampire Bat, it is my nature; I was born this way! So many sweet birds to feed on, so by the time I am done, none will survive to thrive alive, for I'll have eaten everyone! The bloodlust taste I have for their essence of pure life force, starting with fine fluffy Fifi LaFleur served as my main course!"

Magnolia bats her eye lashes at Merlot saying sweetly, "Let's go to the theater dressing room to find costumes to disguise ourselves as Mr. Doom and Mrs. Gloom."

Magnolia and Merlot fly back to the Lucky Ducky Club before heading directly back into the theater dressing room. They both try on different outfits and agree on the black and white Pierrot clown costumes. Merlot puts on a little white pointed hat as Magnolia grabs a form fitted, black beret. The matching vintage clown outfits have wide ruffled collars with long sleeve shirts decorated with pom pom buttons. Magnolia wears a black and white striped skirt while Merlot wears baggy pants. They both paint their faces all white with pancake make-up with red clay and coal black accents around their eyes, brows and cheeks. Merlot paints

a big red smile on his face with a berry beak stick while
Magnolia paints a frown on hers with a tear below each eye.

Merlot turns around toward Magnolia while admiring
himself in the mirror nearby pretending to be snooty, "This
is the perfect disguise as entertainers to be- I wear the
mask of comedy, as you my dear are tragedy."

Magnolia laughs wickedly grabbing a twinkling tiara
made of dazzling diamonds from out of the creaking cabinet
then puts it on top of her head. She proceeds to put on the
black beret fitting it over the tiara snugly.

Magnolia pretends to be sophisticated, "I swear, THIS
will be the temptation that all those ladybirds will want
to wear; it's terribly true, I take after you, that bribery
will get *you anywhere*!"

She laughs once more before turning around to look at
herself in the mirror. Merlot bows toward her before taking
her wing as they both walk off wing and wing out of the
dressing room together.

Fifi and Peony are off backstage engaging in chit chat
when Lazuli comes running over to them. Sage, Rune, Onyx
and Ember hear the flustered fowl so they come closer to
join them. Sage ruffles his feathers and instructs the
baffled birds, "You must *ALL BEWARE* of the big, bad, bat,
for I do not know where he is hiding at. He comes out to
feed at night, in his bloodlust he will try to take a bite!
To drain us *ALL* of our energy source, which is the essence
of our pure life force!"

Putting her wing over her face Fifi says softly, "Oh
how very frightening- This is the worst news I've heard!"

Peony presses her wings together pleading, "I'm glad I
am an early bird, this bat just sounds absurd!"

Onyx points his wings at Rune while saying sternly,
"Rune is the night owl who will watch out for us!"

Lazuli folding his wings calmly replies, "Forewarned is forearmed, so we won't have to fuss."

Ember flares fiery feathers while locking eyes with the other anxious birds, "I WILL WARN YOU ONE AND ALL, IF I DO SEE THAT BAT, I WILL THROW A FIREBALL!"

Magnolia and Merlot see Embers flaming glow in the distance and follow it quietly stopping to hide behind a tree or two in the pine forest. Making their way toward the Birds of Paradise the two wily clown crows join wings waking over to meet the rest of the theater troupe backstage who are startled to see them appear unannounced.

Merlot opens his wings and boasts loudly, "Good day my fine feathered friends, we are Mr. and Mrs. Scarecrow, two singers throwing a new dinner show! Leaving you wanting much more then what you bargained for!"

Magnolia grabs Merlot by his shoulders announcing, "A show of singing, music and dancing with Mr. Crow and me; you all will be entertained to see! We are only here for a short time so I hope you all can come! The show will start three moons from now when the day is done. It's being held between the two hills that match in the bountiful beautiful overgrown pumpkin patch! We are inviting everyone and I'm looking forward to all the fun!"

Merlot dances around all the curious birds waving his wings excitedly, "So all come one, one come all, to the Autumn Pumpkin Ball! On All Hallows' Eve there shall be an event you won't believe! So be there right at violet twilight, where we shall feast under the full harvest moon shining bright, thrown on an eerie evening known as the witch's night!"

Magnolia twirls around with her wings out singing, "All come one, one come all, on the Equinox of Fall! We will have Nature Nectar to drink as the sun begins to sink and the moon begins to rise, the evening will be a big surprise! This is so very exciting to have the whole forest to be inviting! So please make sure everyone comes with you, dress in your finest costume plus wear a mask too!"

Merlot puts one wing up in the air exclaiming, "After the Autumn masked ball shall be the winter festival Evergreen haul! Finding the biggest Pine tree there is to be found, bringing it home to decorate to the music's sound! While we sit, by the Yule log lit, in the fire pit on the ground! With Mistletoe growing out of new fallen snow, you are all invited, so make sure you all will go! We shall have a holiday show to make merry, decking the halls with rows of Holly Berry! Giving gifts of food and drink to one and all, so make sure you make the Fantasy Snowflake Ball!"

Magnolia stops to intone her pitch higher, "On the first day of May is the crowning of Lady Day when all ladybirds shall compete, in the meadow inside Pansflorawood is where we all will meet! The best singer will be crowned the Green Queen, who will parade around in a fragrant flower gown with this diamond tiara here that I found!"

Magnolia takes off her form fitted cap to reveal the twinkling tiara placed on her head. Peony, Lazuli and Fifi look at the diamond tiara with enthusiasm and exhilaration.

Merlot touches Magnolias' shoulders while crooning in a different voice, "Then shall begin the biggest festival of all; The Midsummers' Eve Fairy Festival Ball! The joint will be jumping here in Pansflorawood Glen, to celebrate in summer for the seasons to begin again! There will be food, drink, music and a show. Take your lovebird with you since you are all invited to go! With your birdgent to impress, to the nines ladybirds will dress! All the handsome birdgents will dance with the ladybird they adore; So, don't stay home all alone for that is just a bore!"

The clown crows caw loudly then sing together as one, "We shall celebrate every season in the jubilation of life, come to see our dinner show where you can escape from all of your strife- one life to live, one party to give, the tension can cut like a knife! You will get to know your

55

neighbors, for even strangers can be friends, here is where the fun begins and the music never ends! So all come one, one come all, on the Feast 'O Full of Fall to the All Hallows Eve Ball!"

Merlot takes Magnolia by her wing spinning her around while projecting louder, "With dinner, dancing, a live band and a show, we all love to be entertained- So why don't YOU ALL GO?! Don't forget to be there right at eight, bring your date and don't be late! All come one, one come all, to the Autumn Pumpkin Ball! Come bee, come bug, come bird, COME ALL! We will be sure to entertain you with dining, dancing and drinking; hob nob with the who's who! Remember to be an early bird and come with the whole crew, wear your favorite custom costume and win a prize too! Yooo tooo can be a night owl if you really GIVE A HOOT! With ladybirds dressed to impress in their best! You gents can come in a silk slacks suit! This show is for ALL OF YOU to catch, held in the beautiful, bountiful overgrown pumpkin patch!"

The two clown crows finish their silly acrobatics stunts before turning around and waving goodbye without saying a peep. They vanish as suddenly into the shadows as they showed up.

Ember lights up, "This sounds like a magical delight,"

Lazuli jumps up and down, "We get to dress up in costume for a masquerade night!"

Onyx touches Peony's wing smiling, "To have dinner and drink by the violet twilight!"

Peony spins around and around, "I know exactly what I will wear and how I will decorate my hair!"

Fifi claps her wings happily, "I find the invitation quite apropos!"

Sage shrugs his shoulders and agrees, "Since we celebrate the seasons anyway, why don't we all go?"

Rune salutes before he hoots and hollers, "I think we deserve to go- but *first* it's on with the show!"

Glancing down at the clipboard Ember claps her wings firmly, "Places everyone, it's curtain call for us all, as it says here in the text, line up now for our duets are next!"

CHAPTER 13

Solstice and Equinox

The orchestra booms loudly as all the wide-ranging insects and animals start harmonizing together. *The Birds of Paradise* Thespian Troupe reenter together forming a line all in a row. They emerge holding each other's wings forming a brightly colored rainbow. They all turn to find their partner switching two by two as Rune and Fifi are the first to frolic forward out into the front spotlight:

Rune puts out his wing at the feminine flamingo, "You'll find if you wait, it's never too late- I look forward beyond time, as a path begins to wind, while the lane is narrowly bending, once upon a time is our happy ending!"

Fifi smiles as she grabs his wing, "From the late part of March until the end of spring, we shall dine, dance, laugh and sing."

Rune smiles back grabbing her other wing, "Through the end of April until the end of May, we shall eat, feast, work and play."

Fifi twirls and twists in his wings, "In Flora and Fauna I shall be adorned and crowned; on a throne with a maypole of chicklings spinning round and around."

Rune stops Fifi from spinning as he embraces her, "In your blossom bonnet with all the buds upon it, in the midst of May, you shall be my Queen I crown for Ladybird Day."

The two songbirds join wings together, "We shall celebrate Spring with fragrant flowers, wading in waterfalls created by raindrop showers."

The dancing duo stop to look at each other, "Our courtship is a treasure, while our friendship is a pleasure, as a couple of lovebirds we'll stick together, friends with our other birds of a feather, inside our treehouse within fields of purple Heather."

Fifi comes closer to Rune, "Troubles are only temporary and pass just like a dream, like clouds that cover the sunshine which still continues to beam!"

Rune holds her in his wings staring at her smiling, "We know the joy that true love will bring for Winter never fails to turn back into Spring."

Fifi and Rune dance together while making their way out of the toadstool circle. Lazuli fluffs up his feathers before prancing in with Alabaster preening his close by:

Lazuli flaunts feather fans, "From the late part of June until mid-September we shall reflect to reminisce the best times to remember."

Alabaster puffs out his chest, "Balmy breezes blow with the scent of flowers so sweet, in our fragrant food forest with all kinds of fruits to eat!"

Lazuli poses in the spotlights glow, "The sunshine here is a perfect eighty degrees precise; in this Summerland there's no place like paradise!"

Alabaster hands Lazuli a conch seashell, "All the birds of a feather flock here together because the weathers so nice!"

Lazuli takes the seashell from Alabaster and blows into it, "A cold, conch seashell has an ocean tale to tell, as we sit around the bonfire lit, I inhale the smoldering wood smoke smell."

Alabaster bows and tips his twilled tweed cap, "Flying over the food forest just cloud kissed by raindrops, dripping from fiddle fern fronds in the canopy treetops."

Lazuli clasps his wings together dramatically, "This is a dreamland place, in a sacred space, expressed through healing arts, a place of endless beauty for lonely, broken hearts."

Alabaster places his wings over his heart, "For a love that brings a heart joy or pain, is just like a flower that only grows in the rain."

Lazuli hands the conch shell back to Alabaster, "A rare *peacock* pearl from an oyster in the sea; I shall wear around my neck to call my beloved back to me."

Alabaster takes the seashell back with one wing holding it outward, "Happiness is never out of reach, let's go and eat Abalone on the beach!"

The albino albatross steps back as the proud peacock points to the line of other birds stepping offstage. Onyx and Peony take their turn holding wings while dancing out together into the front spotlight.

Onyx bends to one knee, taking a moment to wink at the Elven Lord before returning full attention to the pretty parrot. He pulls out a golden ring, "Will you marry me Peony as the autumn leaves fall? We shall celebrate our union at the masquerade ball."

Peony accepts the sparkling ring, "Yes Onyx, we will romance around, you in a tux, me in a white silk gown."

Onyx stands up smiling embracing her, "Everything is working out quite nice- but please don't throw any rice."

Peony squawks in delight holding him close, "You are my knight in shining armor who has come mounted high, to love, honor and cherish forever taking me to your treehouse by the sky."

Onyx holds his wings around her waist, "Let's go trick or treat under the full Harvest Moon tonight, like lovebirds living in the limelight."

Peony giggles opening her eyes wider to admire her ring, "Yes, this is true indeed; don't throw rice, only throw seed."

Onyx looks into Peony's wide eyes, "You are the love of my life; I do want you for my wife."

Peony gazes lovingly as she rubs down his head feathers, "Onyx, you're my dream come true; I want to spend the rest of my life with you too."

Onyx glances over to the lord and lady and nods his head, "Everyone here we will be inviting, our wed-binding shall be quite exciting!"

Onyx and Peony kiss each other before dancing out of the center circle together. The spotlight now shines on Sage and Ember who strut up into the front spotlight.

The phoenix blazes her fire feathers brightly, "At the last phase of the year, right before it ends; we will have our Winter gathering of family, food and friends."

Sage stomps around Ember in a circle doing his Pow Wow dance, "We shall sing songs of praises to the elementals above, for giving us this Earth and each other to love."

Ember spins in a circle floating up into the air, "We shall spin in a circle with the orbit of the Earth, recycle, reuse, reduce and renew, the cycle of death and birth."

Sage continues to move around her, "Let us go for a sleigh ride to the igloo of Eskimos, then make angels on the ground when it snows."

Ember turns to face Camellia and Obsidian dancing, "On the Winter Solstice we will throw a yuletide event, with my love birds' family and mine, spend time with my birdgent."

Sage raises his massive wings high up into the air, "From each Solstice to the Equinox as the wheel of the year passes through; we wish you gifts of peace, love and happiness making all your dreams come true."

Ember glows brightly while floating over the crowd with her wings extended outward before Sage flies up to greet her. The Indian Eagle and Hawaiian Phoenix sing in harmony together, "The Nightingale weaves her fairytale of the Earth's clear crystal waters, reflecting like a mirror by the Moon Maidens daughters. Jack in the Green Man sews his seeds within the soil of life, the watcher of the woods with Mother Nature as his wife. He is Old Father Time, with a riddle to rhyme, for a new year to come that is good, enlightenment inside this fairy ring called Pansflorawood!"

I have a wish that I hope will come true- That the Nightingale arrives tonight to come and sing for you!"

Even more cautiously then when he entered Alabaster peers backstage where almost the entire troupe is circled around Peony to look at her new band of gold on her ring feather. Onyx looks over at Alabaster giving him a maritime salute, "Glad your wife let you perform tonight considering it's so far across the sea; I'll give my best on your behalf to the other birds so your absence is not a mystery."

Alabaster nods his approval, "It is a long journey home however I only fly so far, then I catch a ride with the sailor seagulls on a schooner ship known as the Dog Star. We have to fight off the pirate pigeons and sometimes even sharks, to return safely back to my fishing village of Danish Doves and Landlubber Larks."

Onyx laughs and waves, "safe travels my friend I'll be leaving here soon too, say hello to Katie for me and take care sir, toot-a-loo!

The giant Albatross returns the same salute, "toot-a-loo!" He adjusts his cap before flying up into the sky to head back to be with his own lady bird and their homemade houseboat.

CHAPTER 14

Japanese Nightingale

Out of the sky spiraling down in aerial acrobatics is a sparkling silver bird. She wears a kimono of shimmering stars, gliding down to stand still at Embers side. Embers fire feathers flare up brightening the stage in golden light when she unexpectedly sees the Japanese Nightingale.

Ember announces excitedly, "Lord of the Night, Lady of the Light, the final act for tonight is our own euphonious Nightingale- She is quite a sensational sight!"

Ember applauds with the audience then briefly exits backstage. She brings the Birds of Paradise thespian troupe back out as they all sit together forming a half circle in front of the stage to watch the Nightingale's peak performance.

Sakura bows to the royal couple then starts to sing her soprano song, "I am Sakura, named after the Cherry Blossom tree, I will enlighten you if you listen to me. All you have to do chant my name; life as you know it will never be the same. I'll sing a song by soliloquy, serenity of sound, a synchronicity of synergy, purely, perfectly, profound! A musical message you'll see, what is to be will be, your destiny to be a Songbird extraordinary! I have come from Eternal Antiquity to introduce you to the Muses. The first Calliope a mixture of poetry with harmony; a vision of her imagination fills this room, like the fragrance of Jasmine in evening bloom. Shy Euterpe is an inspiration of lyrics, words and rhyme infused with all instruments rhythmically sublime. Melancholy Melpomene sings of only tragedy, a relationship combined of how love is blind but also hard to find. Her gift is to transform a broken heart into a masterpiece of art. Terpsichore can float on point with her dedication to dance, moving across the floor to pose in ballet stance. A quintessence of balance refined, in graceful effervescence, her posture perfectly aligned. Erato can sing a high Soprano song, for it is she who taught me how to hold a note so long.

Polyhymnia paints perfect pictures from dusk until the dawn, she can make an ugly duckling transform into a swan. Urania studies Astrological Astronomy through her telescope, an otherworldly galaxy to see every shooting star, along with passing planets both here, near and far. Then there is funny Thalia a theatrical actress of comedy, jokes and fun, as laughter is the best medicine, she heals everyone. Last meet pretty Clio a playwright on history of battles won and lost; to heroes and heroines with casualties of cost. She writes her stories of victory and loss, trials, tribulations and toils, the goal is the endgame to the vanquisher goes the spoils."

Sakura looks at the shining star on the horizon as she continues to sing, "We all strive for enlightenment, to be happy and content for every day spent. We stay on the path from awareness to realization, carrying on to conscious contemplation. Every day of every season, is happening for a reason. We weave a tapestry of every thought, word and deed it all is interwoven if we fail or if we succeed. Your attitude determines your altitude, so keep your morale high and tall, every thought becomes a prayer if you fly or fall. Splinters of stars like diamond dust cross the heavenly plane, creating clouds to come cover the sun with a downpouring of rain. Thinking for yourself is a living art, look within, follow your heart. Lotus Lilies seed and feed themselves in murky, muddy waters, just like these Muses on Earth who are the Moon Maiden's daughters. We can take you into another place, a new perception in a sacred space. Which Muse will you choose for inspiration, to stimulate your third eyes imagination? This is universal law like gravity, where every soul holds the key to unlock the galaxy. Its law will permeate, while solar systems gravitate, in the planet atoms energy force. When you form vibrational vision, you become the source. Plentiful planets are a cosmic mystery, that drifts through the voids of ancient history. There is a divine plan for every woman and man, all of us have life lessons we should trust- Energy flows where attention goes, the universal law is just. Mesmerize to visualize, fantasize then realize when you finally open your eyes that Life is too short for heartaches; don't waste time being blue, your heart will beat happiness when all that is revealed is true."

Supernaturally Sakura starts to hover while dancing in midair. She slowly floats away out of the fairy ring while still singing, "Take heed from all the birds; your worth is in your words, always look before you leap and your wisdom will be yours to keep. In a flight of fantasy let your soul take wing, an enigma of ecstasy as you begin to sing. So go now count your blessings as I so often do; having intuitive insight, easily empowering love and light through you, peace of mind you will find when you are real and true! Now I'm done, my song is sung, I must say toot-a-loo!"

"Toot-a-loo!" The entire wedding party as well as all the creatures and critters in the audience call out from below.

The encore of clapping and cheering continues as everyone yells, "Miracle!"

Sakura says, "Sayonara" with both her shimmering silver wings waving in the wind as she takes flight slowly disappearing from view into a cloud castle.

CHAPTER 15

Unique Unicorn

Hornbuckle plays a quick fanfare tune on his panpipes as he trots out to stand in the center spotlight.

Honeysuckle glides over to dance around him while waving at the *Birds of Paradise* to all stand up, "Thank you, *Birds of Paradise* for coming to perform for us here, we hope to see you again this same time next year!"

The theater troupe take their final bow before sitting down as once again all the guests applaud and cheer, "Miracle!"

Honeysuckle flutter-flies over to stand at the side of Hornbuckle before waving to the crowd to sit back down again. Even the royal couple seem surprised as they both look at each other. All the gathered guests remain seated as they all look around whispering. The Butterfly fairy motions to the orchestra to begin to play, "We have one more surprise in store for you tonight, orchestra if you will arrange a score alright?"

Hornbuckle announces, "Now the Lady of the light by natural law is protected, while the Lord of the night is cosmically connected. Let us watch them enchant us in love and romance, with their first wed-binding dance!"

Camellia and Obsidian join arms smiling and holding each other as they spin around dancing together in rhythm with the various instruments played by the Flora Fae Fairies and Fauna Wood Elves.

The assembled orchestra starts to play a mystical melody as Honeysuckle sings, "There is a forest over yonder hill where soft breezes churn an old wooden mill. There are Kingdoms with castles owned by Periwinkle Pixies with farms, barns, lakes and streams full of Neon Nixies. We all daydream of tranquility, while we sleep in serenity, as flowers open their petals wide, insects work together side by side."

Honeysuckle floats gracefully over to Camellia giving her a small bouquet of Gardenias and Tuberose smiling, "Stop to smell the flowers, admire the butterflies and bees, help us to save our world by planting more shrubs and trees. Together we shall celebrate the seasons of the year, growing our food forest with the creatures from Pansflorawood here. Flowers bloom all year round, serenading stags all along the ground. As blossoms bloom with fragrance new, they sparkle rainbows in morning dew. Rabbits run across the fields where wild horses lie, all having different colors, sizes, ages and cry. They run across the land of grass to a ground of green, to drink out of the pristine pool and stream. Inspiring your imagination out of a day dream."

Camellia and Obsidian continue to dance around to the magical music sung by the faun and fairy.

Hornbuckle clears his throat to sing, "The unicorn is a horse with a horn. They're stately steeds from tiny too tall, some look like a goat others resemble elk all sizes big and small. Most have silver fur and long curly hair. The males have beards, females a solid white mare. With clear eyes of cornflower blue, they have a sixth sense to see right through you. When they deem you worthy, they'll grant you a wish or two. As the legend of myth is told, from stories of these beasts of old, only a pure maiden can hold; the unique unicorn with a horn of pure gold. When the young maiden climbs on the back of this creature, the unicorn will take her to other worldly realms as a telepathic teacher. She will learn much as they travel the land, until a handsome man comes to take her hand. This is the garden of Pansflorawood, this woodland of which I sing, we perform for the celebration of our Fairy Queen and Elven King!"

Honeysuckle sings out, "We are the generation of this garden, the germination living plants we grow. We survive to thrive alive from the seeds on which we sew. Respecting and protecting our orchards with fruit and nuts trees, making wildflower clover honey from the hives of bees. Living in the land of Luneria, from the daylights sunshine gleam through evenings translucent moonbeam. Encircling

67

within the food forest here, we offer you a present, in
this enchanted dream. Find your way here to our garden
where the *Birds of Paradise* sing, a cycle to circle the
seasons of Summer, Fall, Winter and Spring. You must find
your way to visit today within this fairy ring, here's a
unique unicorn to give to our Queen and King. Tell
Buttercup to giddy up, in this gift to you we all bring."

The Lord and Lady stop dancing when they suddenly see
a yellow unicorn with a solid gold horn trot across the
mossy meadow to prance their way. The beautiful beast
approaches them inside the fairy ring as everyone in the
audience stands up in amazement to get a good look at the
rare sight.

Hornbuckle looks at Lady Camellia and Lord Obsidian
singing, "We are the future of this food forest, our only
garden that we grow, feeding us all in wintertime when cold
blizzards breezes blow snow. We wait until the season of
Spring, when new buds of blossoms bring. Feeding the fruits
for eating in summer delight, to warm us by the Fairy
Festival firelight. As Autumn treetops turn shades of
amber, cinnabar and sassafras, frosted crystals of Winter
move like shards of broken glass."

Honeysuckle chimes, "There will come a time when only
those who grow food will be eating, so start planting today
for time is fading and fleeting. Not every maiden will find
a unicorn steed, if you do not tend to your garden, it will
be overtaken by weed, this life is a bountiful banquet of
which we all feed. Animals and plants are gifts to
appreciate that we really need. Starving in the winter
should not be our fate. A strict reminder to grow a food
forest since time will not wait. This is our gift of this
unicorn, to our lovely Queen and King, for your wed-binding
in Pansflorawood, the garden of which we sing, from all of
us to both of you it's Buttercup we bring!"

Hornbuckle hands the reins of colored ribbons over to
Lady Camellia as she places her hand on the unicorn's head
in a loving gesture. Camellia and Obsidian smile as they
are impressed by the unusual beauty of the shy unicorn.
Buttercup looks at them with a twinkle in her blinking blue

eyes and long lashes. Lord Obsidian and his bride Camellia stand up clasping hands as he helps her onto Buttercups back. Camellias gossamer wings beat together as she lands to sit side saddle. Obsidian then climbs onto the back of unicorn as he sits behind his beautiful wife. They both hold tightly onto Buttercup's ribbons as they wave goodbye to all the woodland forest creatures and say, "Toot-a-loo!"

Their forest friends begin waving back from the fairy ring replying, "Toot-a-loo!"

Camellia raises the lightning wand as Obsidian guides Buttercup to prance off toward the direction of the Pearl Palace now gleaming visibly in the distance. The *Birds of Paradise* once more start to make their way back stage to leave when Camellia's father, Topaz gives a hold up motion with one hand. Topaz and his wife Zinnia approach the troupe carrying fruit baskets. Each large basket holds a tall glass bottle filled with Bumble Bee Nature Nectar which Ember gratefully accepts.

Topaz exclaims, "Thank you *Birds of Paradise* for making us cry and laugh; we present to each of you this Nature Nectar carafe!"

Zinnia nods her head and says, "Enjoy these cherries, cranberries, nuts and assorted seed, for your future travels this will be all you need."

Honeysuckle asks curiously, "Where will you birds be traveling to by the way or is this much needed off time today?"

Ember turns to her saying, "Luckily, we will rest for a day or two and then we have another party to do."

Hornbuckle pipes up, "Do you need another announcer for that venue? Honeysuckle and I would like to attend that one too."

Ember replies softly, "This is something the troupe were invited to attend; you are both too young we will see you *here* again."

Lazuli takes hold of the other basket as he listens to the entire conversation. "Look at the little faun trying to horn in when there is eating and drinking to do, plus we've got to get some sleep tonight so I *must* say toot-a-loo!"

As Ember and Lazuli carefully make their way to the other side of the curtain Peony waves them over and squawks excitedly, "Wait, wait! I've got measurements to take and costumes for the ball to make!"

CHAPTER 16

Nightmare Nightshade

Later, located deep within the center of the vast pumpkin patch, inside a plywood wooden structure with patchwork curtains, Magnolia stands behind an oval table. She's placing the Belladonna bloom with the leaves, stems and a cluster of black berries into a mortar and pestle. As she grinds up the ingredients together it creates a sticky black goo. She walks outside to drop three heaping table spoons of the black goo into a big iron cauldron sitting on top of a fire pit bringing the water in it to a boil.

Merlot walks over to her side sniffing the air and chuckles briefly, "I smell something sinister brewing my dear, the time for the Autumn Pumpkin Ball is almost here."

"We must cast a spell with the flower to enhance its mysterious, potent power. To bewitch the birds into a divination of delight as they drink the Belladonna Brew tonight." Magnolia winks at Merlot grabbing the two gourds that have two red ribbons tied around them, "These contain the Cherry Wine that *the* birds will sip and dine."

Merlot grabs Magnolia from behind and whispers in her ear, "This is the perfect place to do it, so do it now, a spooky space for spell casting, Why don't you show me how?"

They hear the bubbles popping and watch as the steam rises up and out of the iron pot turning into a bird skull. Magnolia smiles smugly, "Hand me the flower Mr. Merlot and I will teach you all you need to know."

At that moment Magnolia hears Bonard and Buster groaning and grumbling as they scuffle up the dirt path toward them. The two gangster geese are carrying an antique Victrola record player made of dark wood with its metal handle crank. They are out of breath as they scrape their shabby shoes on the dry dirt before approaching the meddling magpies.

Magnolia repeatedly points her wing toward the inside stomping her foot angerly, "Place it down behind the stage curtain over there, it just can't go anywhere! Watch where you are going with that you lout! Milton, will you go over there and help those buzzards out?"

Bonard and Buster set the Victrola down over behind the stage as Merlot follows them. Standing next to Buster Merlot points his wing down at the antique record player.

Buster bursts, "Hey, what are you doing with Mister Diavolo's old Victrola here? If he gets mad at us it's *me* you're going to fear!"

Merlot says sternly, "You two are barging in on *my* lady and *my* rendezvous, where I'm teaching her how to Tango and as they say it takes two."

Bonard and Buster look at each other puzzled before they turn to leave. Approaching the door Bonard notices a trunk of costumes that says PROPERTY OF THE LUCKY DUCKY CLUB in big, bold, black letters written on the side of it.

Bonard pipes up, "Say, what's the big idea here Bub? Were those costumes taken from the Lucky Ducky Club?!"

Wondering what the delay is Magnolia now stands in the doorway with her wings on her hips anxiously she states firmly, "Yes, those are all the showgirls costumes I was asked to clean AND since I *am* the maid, I'm supposed to wash them, do you know what I mean? I have to return them back tomorrow promptly by noon, this tells you I've got to wash them here soon!"

Buster waves his wing laughing, "Don't want to delay you with all the work you have to do Miss Snow, so have a good evening now we're off, got to go!"

The gangster geese tip their hats at Magnolia and Merlot before proceeding to walk out the plywood door.

"Get out and don't come back!" Magnolia says sharply.

Merlot ruffles up his feathers, "I'll show those boys whose boss and give them a hard whack! They just better zip their lip, there is nothing worse than a whack job on a power trip!" Merlot lifts his head while sniffing the air, "Magnolia my dear, do you smell smoke in here?"

The two blackbirds rush back outside in time to see the last wisps of black smoke rising up from out of the cauldron. Magnolia stomps over to the oval table where she grabs the remaining black goo and water proceeding to throw the rest of both into the cauldron saying angrily, "This is not as simple as making tea, those *mu-daks* think they will make extra work for me!"

Throwing the glass bottle and pestle aside her tone changes as she looks over at her crow mate shaking her head, "They had to come at the last hour, now I have to re-consecrate the flower! Will you go and get the Belladonna blossom for me, so I can finally brew this batch of tea?"

Merlot takes the dark purple flower from a vase inside then walks back out under the starlit sky to hand it over to Magnolia while she stands over the cauldron. Lifting up both her wings in the direction of the moon. She closes her eyes she recites the intriguing incantation.

Magnolia chants, "Bewitching Belladonna… Pans Flora flower… growing only in the midnight hour. I now evoke your magic power! From the old world of folklore and fable, may you be served upon the table with witchcraft, wort cunning and werewolfery- Each bird will drink your demise to be their destiny. I mix all seeds, buds, root and bark, in with the Cherry Berry Wine to be drunk in the dark. With this Nightmare Nightshade to become Belladonna Brew I've made. We will make a toast together, with all birds of a feather to capture Ember, Sage, Rune, Fifi, Onyx, Peony and Lazuli next, for at the stroke of midnight all the birds will be hexed!"

Magnolia throws the flower into the black brew and mixes her steaming potion with a large wooden spoon. After it comes to a boil Merlot throws water on the fire putting it out. Magnolia takes a long ladle and begins mixing the Belladonna Brew stirring it in with the Cherry Wine.

First, she pours it into one gourd and then into the other before she grabs one gourd with each wing holding them up once more chanting, "With the nightshades influence to mix it well, now intensifies this nightmare spell!" Magnolia looks into the gourd as the black liquid has now turned a beautiful shade of deep burgundy. Magnolia caws three times, "Now that this Belladonna Brew is done, I can't wait to serve it to everyone!"

She continues to cackle wickedly turning around to go back inside the plywood platform. Merlot follows her close shutting the patchwork pattern curtains behind them.

CHAPTER 17

Lucky Ducky Club

Peony begins passing out homemade costumes to all her feathered friends. Handing Ember her outfit first, a ravishing red top and glittering gold pants with a long matching veil. Reaching out to give it to her with both wings, "Elegant Ember is a golden genie tonight, wearing Torch Ginger fabric sparkling brilliantly bright!"

Peony turns to Fifi to hand her a gorgeous gown, "Feminine fanciful Fifi, you are an angel's dream, here's a halo of daisy flowers and a silk lace dress of cream. Wings made from the feathers of a swan, with a tuft of fluff dainty dandelion seeds glued on."

Peony picks up a dark brown, shaggy pile of material and walks over to Sage smiling, "Sage is shape-shifting into a wild wolf with a suit made of muddy moss and furry Paintbrush Plant. From the top of hood right down to the end of the pant."

Next, she retrieves a large iridescent green mound handing it over to the raven, "Onyx becomes the dashing dragon with beetles' iridescence scale, placed one by one from your twig horns to the tip of your tail."

Picking up a pile of accessories she approaches the wise owl, "Rune you are a pirate with a dark bark cloth suit, with these dirty boots on you'll be a real hoot! Here's your belt, buckle and bootstrap, with baggy pants matching this black cross bone cap."

Taking down two hangers from a nearby Elm tree she crosses over to the peacock saying softly, "Luxurious Lazuli, here are some sparkling scarves sheer and wispy; I'm transforming you tonight into a gypsy! A headscarf of coins, fern and feather, the handkerchief dress with different colors is dyed by purple Heather."

Peony steps back, spins around in front of the group referring to her own costume, "I'm going to be a Periwinkle Pixie in this dress of moss and grass, decorated in bluish blossoms with wings made of copper and brass." The proud parrot turns around to show off the detailed wings she made that open and shut.

All the birds disperse into different shrubs and hedges that line the length of the path that leads to the pumpkin patch. They each dress up in their elegant, elaborate costumes. The *Birds of Paradise* wait for the other members of the theater troupe to finish and arrive until everyone is together once again on the snail trail.

Rune points his wing out in the direction of where the Autumn pumpkin ball will be, "The pumpkin patch is past the Shadowlands in the valley down below, where the Hemlock, Hawthorn and Hazelnut trees grow."

Sage yawns, "I hope I can stay up late enough to enjoy the show. I'm not a spring chicken anymore you know."

Ember looks at Sage smiling, "Under an ancient Birch tree, an old wise worm once said to me, *inch by inch, everything is a cinch.*"

Onyx exclaims, "Come on now let's go and quickly make our way, it's almost violet twilight at the end of the day!"

Fifi claps, "I can't wait to see Mr. and Mrs. Scarecrow!"

"What?" Peony squawks, "Are we waiting for? Let's not miss the dinner show!"

Lazuli smirks, "We will get there right on time and we will not be late, I believe those clown crows said that dinner starts at eight."

Diavolo sits perched up on a tall tree nearby.

Watching and waiting while shifting from one foot to the other he fusses anxiously looking for Fifi to show up below. Finally, he hears the thespian troupe approaching as they chit and chat.

He softly speaks, "Fifi- Fifi, can you see me? Miss LaFleur I am your destiny."

Fifi stops to listen as the rest of the bird bunch continue to hurry on down the path without her. The frightened flamingo walks cautiously as she runs to catch up to her friends. She looks high and low to see where the voice is coming from as her name rides on the whispers of the wind. As soon as she steps under the same tree that Diavolo is waiting in, he quickly swoops down, picks her up and carries her off into the evening sky.

Diavolo soars over forgotten forests before landing a short distance from the green doors that leads them both into the Lucky Ducky Club. An upbeat tempo of drums and horns comes blaring out when they open to enter. Inside a large room is a fast-paced piano playing early 1920's era music. Diavolo sees Bonard and Buster on the inside doing their job as his two bully bouncers. Entering into the Lucky Ducky Club while holding Fifi tightly he forces her farther inside. Fifi looks around the sprawling casino watching a gaggle of gangster geese moving around a roulette wheel quacking and honking loudly. Decked out ducks are playing Craps and shooting dice while dolled up dames are dealing cards at various poker and Blackjack tables nearby.

A large banner on the wall reads 'BUCKS FOR DUCKS' as Glamorous goose gals deliver drinks to female flapper fowl chattering with their friends and families. The room is full of dangerous ducks and gangster geese all seated at the white, cloth-covered tables. Both male and female birds are wearing hats and dressed in black and tan except for the men's vests that have a splash of color to them. Two dandy dames dressed in black and blue garters are singing and dancing together on a wooden stage framed by red velvet curtains.

Diavolo turns Fifi in his direction, staring closely into her eyes with a smoldering look that makes her eyes widen, "Welcome to the Lucky Ducky Club that I own, I'm looking for a superstar like *you* to make the name well known. Just so you know, my name is Sangue Diavolo; I'm always around every day of the year, to see that it runs smoothly in here."

Diavolo brings her over to his private dining table with silverware, fine China, painted wine glasses and cloth napkins. They both sit down in the big booth as he looks around for his body guard bullies, Bonard and Buster. Waving his wing at them he manages to get their attention. The two big geese goons block the entrance just as a fancy flapper approaches the table. The goose gal fills Fifi's glass then Diavolo's with a cherry red wine.

Fifi nervously looks up at the server smiling, "What kind of drink is that you're starting to fill?"

The goose gal smiles back, "It's our house specialty Sangue Sangria, it really fits the bill."

Fifi continues to notice her surroundings while trying a sip of Sangria for the first time. Looking around from where they both sit in the dark corner; she notices a color scheme of mostly black walls with dark engraved woods lit up by dim candle light. She's in shock to see the morbid paintings hanging close by mixed with human hybrids, bird skulls and dead trees with dying dandelions.

Fifi glances over at one of the perverse paintings and calmy asks, "I see your taste in art is rather creepy and obscene. Is it a reflection of your character which is sadistic, cruel and mean?"

Diavolo replies laughing, "Why my dear, the dark walls hide you well in here and hold a multitude of sin; it's my own style I call Art Duckko, that creates this ambiance within."

Fifi replies, "I'm afraid your *duck-kor* leaves much to be desired; I think I best be going now- for I'm getting really tired."

Fifi quickly stands up to leave however Diavolo grabs her wing pulling her back down to sit next to him. Holding her around her tiny waist he smiles in her face exposing his sharp pointy teeth, "I would like for you to perform here, because you are such a rare talent my dear. I want you to do a performance tonight- before we both have a bite. So why don't we toast to that? Just you, the music and your handsome brown bat? You are going to love this drink; Sweetheart it will make you tickled pink."

Diavolo picks up both glasses, handing the one Fifi was drinking from back to her. She takes another sip of wine while Diavolo whispers softly into her ear, "That's it Honey, there you go, just have a sip, take it slow."

Diavolo takes a gulp from his painted grape glass smacking his lips, "You're a natural beauty; a cheesecake kind of cutie. We want to see you preen and prance, showing off your fine feathers in a *fan*-tastic dance! The scent of sweet wine so succulently from your lip, so go on Fifi here take another sip."

Diavolo reaches for her glass, putting it close to her mouth, reluctantly she takes another small sip. Diavolo teases her, "Wouldn't you want to be the star of the show? With your name up in lights so everyone will know? It's so tempting and very clear, you're the perfect prim and proper prima donna here! Beauty, brains and body shaped like an hour glass, now is the time to shine. With your figure fully fine inside your fluffy feathers pretty pink. Are you finished with that Sangria wine? Here, let me buy you another drink!"

Fifi hesitantly comments, "Oui… oui merci Mr. Diavolo… I would love to stay with you and dance, or give your show more than a single glance- however, there is a masquerade ball happening now with a chance to find romance."

Fifi finishes the rest of her wine then picks out an orange slice to eat left in the bottom of the glass. The closest goose gal named Kelly sees her glass empty so she brings another pitcher of Sangria to their table. While she refills the glasses Fifi tries to stand up unsteadily. Diavolo grabs her by the wing forcing her to sit back down holding her even closer.

Diavolo openly flirts, "Why are you being so hyperactive? What's the matter, you don't find me attractive? Let's have another drink or two and then you can go. A new number is beginning I want you to star in you know? I think you should see it and give me an answer soon, in the center of *my* theater and this secret dining room."

Diavolo taps his wine glass with hers clinking them together before they both continue to drink. Diavolo boasts, "I shall delight you with dazzling diamonds, gorgeous gowns and the very best to eat. I shall give you your *own* treehouse here- What do you say my sweet? You may start tonight if you like or earlier in the day. Here my dear have another sip of wine; *now* what do you say?"

Diavolo opens the curtains behind him before pointing out the wide window. Fifi sees a tremendous treehouse in the distance covered in Passion fruit flowers right in the middle of a food filled forest. Her eyes widen looking at the abundant orchards full of figs, apricots, peaches and plums. There are over-grown gardens surrounded by rows and rows of various vines of grapes growing as far as the eye can see. Fifi notices every kind of thorny Bougainvillea and Brambleberry bush growing up from along the forest floor. They create thick walls almost as tall as the trees with streams and waterfalls all weaved through. Thinking of the best life she will have living there, she smiles at Diavolo happily taking another sip of her wine.

Diavolo boasts, "That charming treehouse over there is duck-korated in *the most* darling duck-kor, it has a private garden full of fruits, nuts and berries. I ask you who could want more?"

Fifi turns to Diavolo speaking with a slight slur, "I really do have to leave you see; all my friends are still waiting for me. I really have to go you know; I'm leaving now to meet them at another show. As for your offer, I will have to decline. Fifi tries to stand up but she is dizzy and has to sit back down speaking softly, "Oh dear, I'm afraid I've had too much wine."

She tries to stand up again from the table somewhat shaky breathing heavy and rubbing her head. Fifi continues to sway as Diavolo helps her to sit back down again slowly speaking, "Stop now with the huffing and puffing, breathe, take a breath. The way that you are acting is scaring me half to death! I'm thrilled *you've* agreed to staying here; come let's drink to *that* my dear! How do you like my blood red wine? It's named after me a Sangue Sangria, it means Diavolos divine."

Fifi smirks while moving away from him in her seat, "I'm not putting all my eggs in one basket Mister Diavolo, please excuse me but I really do have to go!"

Diavolo stares back quickly grabbing her wing and pulling her right next to him exclaiming, "My lady bird beauty, you're such a cutie! You wouldn't want to miss the show!"

The Vampire Bat clinks his glass hard against hers while the Flamingo flinches picking up her glass apprehensively taking another sip. Diavolo nods to Bonard and Buster who walk over to his table allowing him to stand up and make his way across the room. They both look over at Fifi who looks up at them nervously before putting her glass back down on the table. Diavolo marches over to center stage before turning around while spreading his outstretched wings upward. He whistles at them to be silent then gets their attention by yelling, "THE LUCKY DUCKY IS PROUD TO INTRODUCE TO YOU TONIGHT OUR VERY OWN SOULFUL,

SULTRY, SNAZZY, JAZZY SHOWGIRLS! GIVE THEM A CHEER
ALRIGHT!"

Diavolo claps his own hairy hands excitedly as the red
velvet curtains open. Everyone in the audience wolf
whistles in between the honking and quacking while clapping
and cheering. Fifi claps softly while watching Bonard and
Buster stand at each end of the black booth trapping her
inside the dimly lit corner. Fortunately, Diavolo points at
the green doors and the two goose goons head back to the
club entrance as instructed. Diavolo approaches frightened
Fifi while seductively squinting as she reluctantly refuses
to take another sip of wine. She opens her mouth to say
something to him just as the piano player tickles the keys.

A loud band of ducks and geese chime in playing an
upbeat tune with brass instruments, drums, guitars and
horns with a single saxophone. Two goose showgirls come out
of stage right and two out of stage left each bird swinging
her hips right into the center stage spotlight. All of them
are wearing matching hot pink and black one-piece outfits
accented with long gloves, French garters and large pink
bow covering their feathery tails. Each showgirl is holding
a big, round, pink powder puff that they use in sync while
dancing together.

The band plays on as the showgirls sing: "Why don't
you powder my back Big Poppa? Powder my back! Come get me
out of my house, the dishes need doing, the laundry is
strewing and my spouse is a louse! I need a dapper daddy to
take me out on the town, to wine me and dine me in my fancy
gown! I shall dress up just for you in my diamonds and
pearls, so I will be the envy of all of the girls. Then you
can show me off at parties held by Barons and Earls!"

Diavolo flirts with the showgirls by winking and
waving as they pass by his table. Fifi takes notice of the
dancing showgirls' tight-fitting outfits and the way
Diavolo is ogling them. She crosses her wings and pouts
turning her head looking the other way.

The showgirls continue to sing, "Powder my back Big
Poppa; powder my back! The bathroom needs cleaning, the
clothing needs sewing, crazy seems to be the only place I
am going! So, take me out Big Poppa, buy me a mink! A
chiffon gown all in soft pastel pink! Take me downtown in
your limousine- to the place that serves the finest
cuisine. Take me out to the best Broadway show, then off
for cocktails and dancing we will go. I deserve it Poppa
for I'm so good to you; I know you want to make me happy
too. Please powder my back Big Poppa, powder my back!"

Every showgirl steps offstage into the audience to
hand a selected birdgent their powder puff to pat on their
bare back. One showgirl gives her powder puff to Diavolo,
who hits her in the tail feathers with it. Seeing this Fifi
begins to guzzle down her whole glass of wine. When the
glass is empty, she waves down the nearest goose gal to
come refill her glass again.

The showgirls collect their powder puffs from all
the grabby gangsters sitting at the tables before
proceeding to strut back up on stage. The showgirls
harmonize, "So now that it's me that you've got, let's go
sail on your yacht! Take me into the city, buy me lipstick,
make me pretty. Boredom only brings the blues; I really
need a new pair of shoes! I'm all dolled up just for you in
my gorgeous gown, put on your tux and tails, let's go paint
the town! We'll party all night long from the dusk until
the dawn. When the night is done, we'll welcome up the sun.
Now that I'm dressed in my nighties of pink and black, just
be a good Daddy and powder my back!"

Diavolo tries for a kiss from Fifi with his lips
puckered. First, she hides her mouth in her feathers but
then she slaps him so hard across the face that it knocks
his fedora hat right off his head. As he gets up to
retrieve his hat from the floor, he spits out several pink
feathers.

Diavolo grabs Fifi's wings roughly as she tries to get
away however he succeeds at pulling her back to sit next to
him. With a serious tone in his voice, he angrily grabs

her, LOOK YOU flamingo floozie, I didn't deserve that shot in the chops!"

Fifi struggles in his grasp replying, "YOU won't take NO for an answer so this is how it STOPS!"

Fifi notices Bonard and Buster looking at her, while trying to escape from Diavolos' hairy hands. The showgirls continue to dance on stage forming a chorus line while waving their powder puffs high over their heads.

The showgirls sing on, "You can take your wristwatch and top hat, your new suit and Cadillac, eat caviar, smoke a cigar, use up all your charm. To the nines I will dress, for you to impress, just don't forget who's on your arm! You treat me like the doll that I am while I'm dressed all in pink and black, now that you've got your dancing shoes on Poppa, powder my back!" The showgirls end in a pose turning around with their powder puffs on their backs.

Kelly brings a pitcher of Sangria back with her to serve Diavolo and Fifi again. By now Fifi is feeling the spinning effects of the wine as she watches the gorgeous goose gal fill up the two glasses. She shakes her head as if to say that's enough before she swiftly stands up at the table, "Oui oui merci monsier, now I AM sure I DO WANT to live in that tree, so give me a chance to show you MY DANCE, I can do this RIGHT NOW WATCH ME! I shall fan dance for you in mon mystique and GIVE YOU ALL A PERFORMACE THAT IS MOST MAGNIFIQUE!"

Diavolo replies back seductively, "I'm such a sucker for pretty things, I'll be here my dear waiting in the wings."

All the eyes in the club are on Fifi now when she projected her words loudly over audience of sitting ducks. The lanky Flamingo is a bit wobbly as he frees her wing to saunter her way over to the piano player swaying her hips. The ducks and geese wolf whistle in the audience while She starts to walk slowly across the room. One of the gangster geese tried to goose her as she walks by so she runs up and grabs the glass of water placed next to a yellow gosling mug holding gold coins wearing a sign that reads TIPS FOR CHICKS. She quickly gulps down every drop before placing the glass down on top of the carved wooden piano.

Winking at the dapper duck who tips his hat winking one eye back at her. Fifi snatches up his ostentatious hat, switching out her angel halo placing it on her head.

"Excuse me, Mister Piano Player but *this hat* belongs on one fancy egg-layer!"

Clyde, the piano player replies, "These goose gals and ganders like honky-tonk rock; dressed up dapper ducks dance all around the clock!"

He nods on cue the other band members who all start playing a rock and roll tune together joining in on their drums, guitars and horns with the saxophone picking up the pace.

Diavolo runs out into center stage waving his wings shouting, "A NEW PERFORMANCE TONIGHT! I WOULD LIKE YOU ALL TO TAKE A BITE! STAND AND WELCOME THE FEMININE, FUN AND FLIRTY, FINE, FLUFFY FIFI LAFLEUR! SINGING WITH OUR VERY OWN SHIP HITS THE SAND BAND!"

The audience claps, cheers and wolf whistles while the crowd watches her dance slowly and sensually trying to keep her balance while moving up onto the stage. Fifi stops to stand in the middle of the decked-out dames all staring at her wide eyed in surprise and shock. The four showgirls are envious of her beautiful pale pink feathers and fair face. Acting annoyed by her unexpected intrusion the dandy dames all stare at her silently while swarming around her like hornets.

All eyes in the club stop what they are doing to watch, wait and see what happens next. Diavolo smiles and taps his hand on the table to the rhythm of the beat.

The French Flamingo begins to dance across the stage while showing off her angelic feathers making them appear bigger than they are. She gives each showgirl eye contact before facing the audience singing,

"Pardon my French but I don't give a fig, if you all want to stare at me while I dance my jig! I'm a long-legged lady looking for my King of Hearts, I've no desire for the Jack of Diamonds that steals all the tarts! It is wrong for you to hate; I only love therefore CHECKMATE! I want a man playing with a full deck not sticking a feather in his cap, you better play your cards right, I'm not falling for your TRAP!

One of the showgirls standing next to her named Nicky is scowling at Fifi with her white wings on her hips screaming loudly, "YOU'RE NOT THE STAR HERE, OUR SHOW YOU JUST WRECKED, NOW YOU WILL BE PUNISHED BY BEING HEN PECKED!"

Fifi tries to stand up her toes to appear taller than Nicky but hobbles back down to stand flat on her feet. The audience claps and cheers for the pretty pink bird lady.

One of the gangster ganders was making more noise than most of the crowd consistently honking and heckling.

A dapper duck calls out, "Hey honkler zip your lip!"

The goose guy gets louder, HEY QUACKER TAKE ANOTHER SIP!"

Fifi quickly steps away from the mean looking showgirls singing,

"I'm a long-legged lady, I've got an ace up my sleeve, I'm not trying to stay here, I've been trying to leave! I realize you have snake eyes and YOUR roll of the dice is NOT VERY NICE! It's true love doesn't pay the rent; I'm just looking for the right bird gent! I'll feather my love nest with the birds and the bees, so back up and back off if you please. On a wing and a prayer, I will find the right chap, I'm not falling for your CRAP!

Another showgirl Tawny glares at Fifi and sarcastically sings, "Uh oh there she goes, she can't even stand up on her toes! We know a good seed from a bad egg, so why don't you go BREAK A LEG!"

"THAT CHICK DOESN'T HAVE A LEG TO STAND ON!" One gander hollers out at Tawny while the audience laughs.

"STOP WITH THE WISE QUACKS! LET HER SING HER SONG!" Another duck yells back at him as the room becomes silent.

"I'm a long-legged lady and prefer afternoon tea, to a gallon of moonshine, that mess does *NOT* interest me. I'm a goodie goodie brought up in upper society, taking care of my health is my first priority. I'm awake at dusk and asleep at dawn, you wouldn't know a lady that's why you want me gone! My complexion is pretty peaches and cream, you see I'm an angel, I AM every man's dream! My feathers are clean see how they glitter and gleam?! Strictly sweet and sassy, a REAL lady that's clever and CLASSY! I'm a RARE BIRD, a lovely lass. I know you don't know, I'm auditioning for the show, SO SAP OFF MY SASSAFRAS!"

Jenny struts forward looking out into the audience of laughing and smiling ducks and geese who are all clapping and cheering. "DON'T BE FOOLS, she's had TOO MUCH to DRINK! When she's sober, SHE'S A BORE, THIS BIRD BRAIN CAN'T EVER THINK! Can't stand up and THAT'S A FACT, this poor thing CAN'T EVEN ACT!"

Fifi is insulted and irritated by the showgirls' words and quickly retorts back, "Lay all your cards on the table and you may get a full house even with this trainwreck! I'm not taking advice from anyone not playing with a full deck! A prison place really is for the birds who live in this gilded cage, YOU ARE ALL JUST JEALOUS OF ME AND CAN NOT CONTROL YOUR RAGE! DO NOT egg-aggerate my talents if you have a bone to pick, for your heart is made of stone and your HEAD IS BIG AND THICK! I don't care if you think I'm

here to steal YOUR show, I thought I would be staying, NOW
I really have to GO! I'TS YOUR LOSS LOOSEY GOOSIES if you
want to sneer and snap, I THINK YOU ALL SHOULD JUST SHUT
YOUR YAP!

    One of the gangster ganders stands up in his chair and
calls out, "YOU BETTER NOT EGG HER ON!"

    Another gander sitting at a nearby table points at
Nancy, "YEAH! WHEN HER FEATHERS GET RUFFLED, SHE FIGHTS
JUST LIKE A SWAN!"

    The audience laughs loudly honking and quacking loudly
as everyone including Diavolo joins in with the others by
clapping and all standing up out of their chairs. The big
bad bat grins grimly as he watches the entertaining
entanglement with wide eyes deviously drooling.

    The meanest showgirl Nancy, walks right up in front of
Fifi screaming, "YOUR WORD IS YOUR WORTH AND YOU CAN'T TALK
YOUR WALK! YOU CALL THAT SINGING, ALL YOU DO IS SQUAWK! HOW
DARE YOU COME IN OUR PLACE THINKING THAT YOU CAN MOCK! NOW
I'M GOING TO HAVE TO CLEAN YOUR CLOCK!"

    The four showgirls move in quickly around Fifi from
all sides trying to hide her from the eager audience that
roars with laughter and wolf whistles. They move ever
closer crowding around her as they all grab onto her wings
trying to take her off stage. Fifi can hardly breathe as
the showgirls close in on her causing her to gasp for air
before she faints. Half of the audience stands up hooting
and hollering while throwing gold coins onto the stage. The
smiling showgirls see all the money and free Fifi as she
flops into a crumpled heap in the middle of the stage. The
sultry showgirls blow kisses to their audience in
appreciation before collecting all the coins. Bonard and
Buster run over to Diavolo who is still laughing and
clapping at his table.

    Bonard exclaims excitedly, "HEY BOSS! That sweet cookie
there is going to MAKE US A LOT OF DOUGH! I think you
should HIRE HER to be the NEW STAR OF THE SHOW!"

Buster chuckles, "That beautiful bird wants to leave? Don't let her go! Look at all the MONEY THESE PLAYERS THROW!"

Bonard rubs his wings together saying, "WE'LL ALL BE RICH! Don't let her fight or flight! You should have HER HERE working every night!"

Buster looks over at Fifi passed out on the floor and mentions, "Too bad she has two left feet, she couldn't even keep up on her own beat. Who cares if she can't sing a tweet! LOOK, everyone is standing up out of their seat!"

Bonard winks at Diavolo asking, "Do you know if that bird babe is seeing anyone? She looks like she'd be a lot of fun."

Diavolo is obviously not impressed by his bodyguard's enthusiasm. He stands up furiously picking up an empty bottle and shakes it back and forth while glaring at the two greedy geese. Trying to keep his composure he shakes the wine bottle at them yelling, "DON'T BE SO QUICK TO PLACE THAT BET, I HAVEN'T DECIDED IF I WILL HIRE HER YET! YOU QUACKPOTS DON'T WANT EGG ON YOUR FACE BY THE TIME I'M THROUGH- I'll CRACK A HARD ONE OVER YOUR HEAD BECAUSE THE YOLK'S ON YOU!"

A single intoxicated disoriented duck is sitting at the bar blowing on a single trumpet trying to drown out Diavolos shouting. The big, bad bat hurries over to stand over Fifi with his wings wide and stretched open crying out, "GET BACK EVERYONE GIVE THIS BIRD SOME AIR!"

Nancy snaps back, "WHY DON'T YOU GO BACK AND SQUAT IN YOUR CHAIR!"

Diavolo angrily runs out of the shadows and stops in front of Nancy scolding her firmly while barking out orders, "WELL NANCY, DON'T JUST STAND THERE! GO FETCH A GLASS OF WATER! DON'T JUST GAPE AND STARE!

When Nancy realizes it's Diavolo and not some honking heckler from the audience she responds, "I'm Sorry, I didn't know it was you boss, I didn't mean to make you so cross."

Diavolo scowls at Nancy as she walks away from him, "HEY, I don't want YOU to start a fight, this is MY Lady Luck tonight!"

The big bad bat hurries over to claim his pretty pink prize. The villainous vampire kneels over Fifi while looking out into the silent audience of curious dapper ducks, flapper fowl, gangster ganders and dandy dames.

Diavolo screams, "I DON'T NEED YOUR HELP! I can do this alone, but before I take this bird here home, I'm going to throw you boys a bone, tell you of a scary spot about a mystery unknown. While we're going to a place of rest, back to her own little tidy nest. There's a Masquerade Ball going on you all need to catch, being thrown RIGHT NOW in the overgrown pumpkin patch! Serving a five-course dinner with drinks and a show, put on a mask and costume, then you all may be free to go- Except for you five goose gals I'll need you to cocktail the show. Grab all the trays and glasses and go find Mister Merlot! There's still more to do and lots to be done- *Then* we can have our fun."

The villainous Vampire Bat rubs his sharp claws together as he watches the goose gals giggle before they turn around and enter into the sand stone kitchen. Filling their suitcases full of napkins and glassware from the cabinets the giddy girls all cackle coupling together as they exit out the entrance. All the other ducks and geese put on their hats and coats before filing out of the Lucky Ducky Club. The last gangster goose shuts the doors leaving Diavolo alone with only Fifi and his two bully bodyguards.

Diavolo calls them over, "Bonard! Buster! I don't know why I was seeing red; I don't even know what I might have said."

Buster looks at Fifi concerned asking, "She hasn't moved for a while, is she dead? NOW HOW WE GONNA GET AHEAD?!"

Diavolo waves his wing motioning them to get closer to listen as he states seriously, "Got something to tell you boys, seems the eagle and the owl have been making *a lot* of noise! They're telling *tall tales* all over town, in an attempt to shut the Lucky Ducky down! They may *even* try to come in here to find *me*, you'll keep watch for them under the nearest tree! Keep your eyes and ears open for anything they might do or say; *shoot* them should they get in the way!"

Bonard touches the slingshot on his hip and boasts, "We'll wait for them and won't be alone, make sure we kill two birds with one stone."

Looking at Diavolo Buster laughs honking, "We'll finish up here then we'll head to the show, but first we *must* get all our ducks in a row."

The three of them exit outside while carrying Fifi in their arms. A giant scruffy Blood Vulture with crusty feathers waits for her owner as she hides in the shifting shadows.
Her eyes glow red when she finally sees Diavolo and the two gangster geese exit out of the green doors she emerges silently and waits. The three of them struggle to place Fifi on the back of the crimson creature who is standing still while watching them. Diavolo climbs on next to Fifi giving the sticky feathers a tug as a cue for the bald bird to fly up into the dark dreary sky.

CHAPTER 18

Autumn Pumpkin Ball

Merlot places a couple of new logs on top of the firepit. He warms his wings before cleaning out the inside of the large black cauldron for Magnolia.

"In order for the birds to dine, I had to hurry and get the fire on time," Merlot explains nodding his head.

Magnolia winks back her approval, "Whatever it takes to keep those birds off their game, if Diavolo fails it won't be *us* to blame."

Merlot flies off, returning on the ground pushing a wheelbarrow full of small pumpkins over to the oval table. He sits down on a wooden stool and proceeds to cut the pumpkins in half then scoops out their innards with a large spoon placing them in a large black iron cauldron.

Magnolia takes the two gourds full of Belladonna Brew, holding one gourd in each wing she lifts them up toward the moon chanting, "Never underestimate the power of a flower, for as it grows, its wisdom knows, the blossom on the bower. Let this potent, poison, potion infuse under this full moon spell, creating an illusion of confusion, where these birds can never tell. On All Hallows Eve they shall fall into a deep sleep, then the food forest shall be mine to keep. Imagining their dream is really a nightmare, when it seems a pleasant delight, on this eerie evening known as the witch's night."

The two Magpies cackle and caw before returning back inside to set up tables and chairs out by the stage.

Merlot looks around at the makeshift theater with its plywood platforms stage and patchwork patterns curtains.

He smirks before stating, "Well my dear, it may end up to be standing room after all,"

Magnolia smiles, "Once upon a time at the Autumn Pumpkin Ball."

Walking back to place one of the gourds on the decorated tables she turns her head to ask, "Now where on Earth is Mr. Dingbat; do you know where he is seated at?" She rolls her eyes quite disgusted.

"I don't know where he would go; he knows tonight is the night of the show. Still things left over to do; I'll start to warm up the stew." Merlot hurries over with a wooden spoon to stir the bubbling brew.

The boisterous British butler takes off his derby hat before he heads back outside to the oval table picking up one bucket of pumpkin innards as well as another bucket holding assorted insects. He throws them in alive into the iron cauldron and stirs them all in together. Walking back to the table he picks up two big bottles of water, emptying them into the piping hot cauldron. He goes back and forth to the nearby river to use the rushing water for food and drinks they both create. He stirs in 9 Wolfsbane blossoms into the brew once again before walking back inside toward the dressing room created out of giant palm leaves and thick branches.

Once inside he begins to wrap himself up in strands of long dirty fabric to look like a mummy. After an hour he exams himself at all angles in front of the broken mirror chuckling to himself how realistic he appears.

"I'm all wrapped up in the perfect disguise; look my dear you can't even see my eyes. Good thing the club had all our needed supplies; nobody would guess we really are just a couple of magpies."

"I threw all the black goo into the pot," Magnolia laughs.

"Now we'll just have to wait for the brew to bubble hot," Merlot raises his fluffy brows and sniffs the air.

"Soon we shall have our own little nest egg back in our own Oak tree, the one in the food forest that you built only for me." Magnolia flirts as she blows him a kiss.

Merlot walks over to put a record on the Victrola player and plays an upbeat Latin jazz song with blaring, horns, guitars and drums. He approaches Magnolia with his wing out, "Magnolia… you are love of my life, I do so want you for my wife, you deserve only the best, I will do everything in my power to get back our little love nest."

He embraces her around her waist before they both begin to dance a tantalizing Tango in sensuous silhouette under the moons shadow.

A short time later they can hear the *Birds of Paradise* chittering and chattering in the distance. Merlot peeks out of the dressing room curtain to see the creatures and critters of the forest start to arrive. The thespian bird troupe are starting to take their seats as they approach the largest empty table of 12 seats marked RESERVED. A few minutes later taking other tables in the surrounding area are some of the flapper fowls, gangster geese, dapper ducks and dandy dames from the Lucky Ducky Club. Merlot fakes a smile looking at all the excited birds flocked together.

"I don't want this to ruin our big night however; I do not see Fifi here anywhere in my sight." Merlot looks back at Magnolia, his eyes go wide and he speaks in a concerned tone, "I think Diavolo took Fifi too soon for his fun, when she is supposed to be here *now* with everyone!"

"I'm afraid the fox is in charge of the chicken coop, that DINGBAT is a complete nincompoop!" Magnolia places her wings on her hips as she taps one foot anxiously.

"Well let's not count our chickens before they hatch." Merlot sighs, "*She* has to be here somewhere in the pumpkin patch. We better think of a new plan fast or the birds here are not going to last."

Magnolia raids through the trunk of circus costumes, trinkets and tidbits, "Fear not, no need to fret. We are *not quite* done here yet! I know what I *must* do! I'll dress up like Miss LaFleur and mimic and mock her too!" Magnolia continues to rummage through the various hats, masks and colorful clothing.

Merlot briskly walks over opening a square box of many props while throwing gizmos and gadgets out of it onto the floor, "Thanks a lot my dear, we've opened up a big can of worms here! Do you think those bird brains out there will see you as a fake?

Magnolia briefly glares at him, "I don't care as far as I'm concerned THIS IS MY BIG BREAK!" She struts across the room to the trunk where she quickly begins removing more cute costumes from out of it onto the table.

Merlot has a realization, "Even under this moon light, we're going to have to make you proper height- Thus far I have found only a broom and mop, to be Fifi's size I'm afraid you will have to hop."

"I know what I can be; this black cat suit fits me perfectly! Go! Hurry! Announce me now, MEOW, this plan we can't afford to blow, that Miss Lafleur is now part of *our new* show!" Magnolia proceeds to put on the cat costume and attach the mop and broom as improvised stilts to her legs.

Merlot ties them to Magnolias' feet with a thin robust reed ribbon winking at her, "Good thinking my dear, we have no reason to fear."

Magnolia points her wing out of the dressing room exit as Merlot rushes quickly into center stage yelling loudly, "Dapper ducks and dandy dames, please have a seat! Goose gals pass out dinner and desert! Get ready for a trick and a treat! With Harvest stewing and spirits brewing with All Hallows ween spice! This next number is just for the extraordinary Birds of Paradise! We have a special guest tonight, to sing and dance for you, MAESTRO Miss Fifi Lafleur without further ado!"

One of the dangerous ducks who has already drunk a whole bottle of Sangria wine sees Suzy and slurs his speech, "Hey Sweetheart! How's about refilling my cup?!" Grabbing the small pumpkin decoration off his table he throws it in Merlot's direction, "Hey Quackpot! When are you going to wrap this up?!"

The audience laughs at Merlot while he exclaims excitedly, "I am Mr. Peppercorn Scarecrow! I'm here to host tonight's *spook*tacular show! I've come to welcome you one and all to the Autumn Pumpkin Ball! Where bats, bugs, bees and birds come to hear mysterious words! To feast away the day, then dance the night away, this All Hallows Eve of fright! Bugaboos and boogaloos in bioluminescent flights fly by with ethereal entities of elemental sprites. With all you ladybirds and birdgents dressed up to parade for the charade of the midnight masquerade! Here in this pumpkin patch, you will experience many sights, as we razzle dazzle setting the stage in orange and purple lights! This is the most solemnly, sinister night, with the full Harvest Moon as our only spotlight." Suzy gives Merlot a goblin goblet of vine wine in his right wing to hold up to the heavenly glowing orb.

Another gangster gander stands up out of his chair shouting, "MAYBE IT'S THE STEW OR MAYBE ITS JUST YOU! MY STOMACH IS STARTING TO CHURN, NOW GO AWAY AND GIVE THAT THERE SHOWGAL A TURN!"

Merlot ignores the feathered feedback from the honking heckler expressing his enthusiasm, "With our Goblin goblets let's make a toast together, on this eerie evening my fine friends of a feather! That we finish what we set out to do, with gratitude and sacrifice we will be successful too! Now lets' get down to the nitty gritty here's Miss LaFleurs' first number called *Here Pretty Kitty*! With an entrance that is both great and grand- Won't you all please give Miss Fifi LaFleur a hand?!"

All the Birds of Paradise clap politely as Merlot drinks a sip of his goblet before handing it back to Suzy. He turns around and runs quickly between the patchwork curtains to go backstage where he begins to crank the handle on the old Victrola player. The arm comes down to play a record as the speakers blast out an upbeat roaring twenties time tune. Merlot peaks out from behind the curtain motioning for a couple of goose gals to join him backstage. He hands Suzy and the others trays with the gourds full of the Belladonna Brew.

Merlot speaks in his deadpan voice, "Pay careful attention to my word, take these to that table there the one with the flaming Firebird."

Suzy saunters her way over to table where Sage, Rune, Onyx, Peony, Lazuli and Ember are sitting. Merlot hands out more goblets on a tray to the other goose gals telling them to pass out the drinks to the rest of the gangster geese, dangerous ducks and fancy flapper fowl.

Rune takes a goblet from the beautiful ladybird as he looks up at her flirting, "This is a dream I never want to wake up from."

Onyx receives a drink as he smiles, "I'll be sorry when the ball is done."

Sage watches Suzy places a goblet down on the table in front of him perking him up, "I hope I don't fall asleep and miss out on all the fun." He yawns as she walks away.

Lazuli looks at Suzy putting down his goblet on the table top in front of him. He sniffs the air looking around to see all the other goose gals and gathered guests filling goblets with gourds. He notices a long log table full of fresh fruits, vegetables, desserts and a gigantic pumpkin hollowed out to hold more Harvest Stew. He closes his eyes and inhales deeply saying, "Oh my, Apples, peaches, pumpkin pie, Harvest Stew, Hallows Brew, Cinnamon Cider and Chai!"

Merlot once more peeks out of the patchwork curtains as Magnolia finishes getting dressed in her cat costume standing behind a twisted twig screen. Merlot speaks softly, "I see all the *Birds of Paradise* sipping on their drink; soon they will be so dizzy that they can hardly think." He turns around just as Magnolia steps out from behind the screen.

"They think they are so smart believing they are free, why they're just a slave to the grindstone and as stupid as can be!" She caws wildly as she grabs a pastel pink feather boa to wrap around her body matching Fifi's pink feathered tutu.

"Miss Magnolia, you look divine! Now here we go it's show time! Let's do our best to entertain them, I'll divert the women, you distract the men." Merlot cranks the handle of the record player again slower as the sound of a single cello plays a melancholy melody. He rubs his wings together and peers out of the curtains with one eye.

Magnolia adjusts her pale pink wig and black cat mask then finishes her costume with a pair of cat ears on her head. She spins her cat tail around in a circle while flirting, "I bet this treat of a number will get all of them to look, after all bread and circus is the oldest trick in the book."

Merlot pulls at the ropes as the stage curtains open. The audience applauds from the flapper fowl and dandy dames when they see the black cat actor. Clapping loudly and howling wolf whistles at her the gangster geese and dangerous ducks drink their moonshine. Creatures and critters clap and cheer. It's hard to see Magnolia when she appears onstage since she only has orange and purple lights to illuminate her.

A brass tuba toots out a tune before Magnolia begins to sing while mimicking Fifis' voice, "*I am Soween an All*

Hallows black cat, looking for my handsome Vampire Bat, to take me out for a midnight cap. I will jump on his back, to ride into a sky so black, we'll glide. As we fly past stars of the Milky Way, into the storm clouds grim and gray. Where thunder rolls and lightning strikes, dark mountains so steep, flying over valleys of rocky cliffs deep. We'll fly by the home of Crane, Heron and Loon, where the Werewolf howls by the big, blue, full moon. Passing over the Oak, Ash, Birch and Yew, where orchards have apples of blossoms anew. Over corn crops and pumpkins with large leaves unfurled, he flies me to spooky spaces all around the world. As spiders are writers that give me a fright and all other shadows that go bump in the night."

Lazuli looks toward Sage with a suspicious frown. He crosses his wings as well sarcastically he snaps, "I warned you *all* what he's capable of; it isn't like he's some pure peaceful dove! I find it very ironic that Fifi is singing about a Vampire Bat."

Sage yawns again looking back at the singing, costumed character on stage then replies, "Yes, I find it strange as well, Deja' vu in fact."

Peony shrugs her shoulders squawking, "It sounds like Fifi singing, I suppose."

Ember leans in to get a closer look, "Well, if it is, she isn't even on her toes."

Rune turns his head in all directions. "It looks like a flamingo dressed up like a bewitching black cat."

Onyx places one wing against his forehead squinting, "Yes, but it's hard to tell this far back."

All the birds continue to drink the Belladonna Brew as the goose gals come around to refill their goblin goblets. While still other goose gals bring more pumpkin bowls of Harvest Stew to their table. The birds eat, drink and laugh as they enjoy themselves and the All Hallows live music.

Magnolia continues her soulful singing, *"In his sharp dressed suit and spats, he flies around chasing cats. In his tuxedo he likes to dress for all the pretty kitties to impress.*

We fell in love at first sight; we see each other every night. He knows how to treat me right, when takes me out on a midnight flight. Supernatural and nocturnal just like me, we drink, we dance, we hug, we kiss, he makes me so happy! I fell in love just on a whim; I really can't get enough of him! Every day I love him more and more, as we Tango across the floor. He is so refined as his wisdom grows; he really knocks me off of my toes!" In an attempt to spin Magnolia nearly loses her balance in the stilts.

Gaining her gravity she sings, *"With his cape like wings and tall top hat, he is my handsome Halloween Bat! He flies me over marshland swamps of moss and misty fog, sitting down beside me with a freaky frog on a log. Surrounded by Spruce where birds fly by and chirp; to the sound of toads that all around us burp. Ghostly orbs like flickering lamps are near, fading out before they reappear. It's the legend of the jack-o'-lantern so I'm told, guarding the buried treasure of the Bog Goblin's pot o' gold. When you see this Phantom foolish fire come to you then go away, it will take you off your path leading all astray. When my man takes me to spooky spaces around the world, he makes me feel like I'm his very special girl!"*

Rune glances over at Sage seeing him slumped over the table fast asleep. Looking around the group, he sees they are all heavy-eyed. He yawns as he tries to keep his eyes open himself, "I think it's time for all of us to go, I feel like sleeping now too you know?"

All the birds fall asleep one by one at the table, Rune being the last one to close his eyes. The one gangster gander now turns his attention to the sleeping, snoring birds.

The honking heckler mocks, "Looks like those bird brains drunk too many jugs, guess they all got bitten by bed bugs!"

A dashing duck walking by his table hears him and remarks, "They couldn't handle the drinks they had. Hey that blue green one isn't half bad."

Magnolia sings seductively, "*I find him so compelling- With his spellbinding storytelling, flying over a dark storm brewing, he tells me of ghosts and ghouls construing. The black clouds kiss the mountain tops goodbye, as he brings me back to my treehouse in the sky. He flies off and calls out from way up above, arrivederci pretty kitty it's only you that I love!*"

The music ends and Merlot takes the arm off the record allowing it to slow down and stop as the stage goes dark. Magnolia struts back to the dressing room where Merlot waits for her with his wings crossed. He shakes his head flailing his feathers flustered and furious, "You shouldn't have mentioned about a Vampire Bat!"

Magnolia snaps, "Don't get your feathers ruffled, it rhymed with cat, besides a rat, I just couldn't do that!"

"You should *never* tip your hand!"

"With the deal I was dealt I thought you'd understand!"

"I still think to mention a bat was wrong!"

"I had to make it up as I went along!"

Realizing his yelling could wake the sleeping troupe Merlot peaks out of the curtain, "The birds are still asleep! They weren't even suspicious, we made sure that Belladonna Brew was delicious!"

Merlot jumps in the air as Magnolia gets up to see for herself that the birds are all still asleep at the table. She smiles smugly in seeing that their plan has worked.

Urgently Magnolia says, "Get the ducks and geese to help you carry Rune, Onyx and Sage to Mariner's Cave at the tip of the cape; block the entrance with big boulders so they cannot escape. Take Lazuli and Peony to Gallows Grove to the old Oak tree.

Lock them inside, with branches to hide, so they cannot break free. I will take care of Ember, leave her up to me."

Moments later Merlot gets some wily geese and willing ducks to quietly help him carry off Sage, Rune, Onyx, Lazuli and Peony out into the overgrown pumpkin patch.

Magnolia passes out garden gloves to three other goose gals to help her pick Ember up, place her into a wheelbarrow and quietly cart her away.

CHAPTER 19

Mermaid's Mirror

Sage groggily starts to awaken as he fell asleep even before he had a chance to finish all of his Belladonna Brew. Looking around in the shadows he sees Rune and Onyx in what appears to be a cave and they are both sleeping.

Sage cries out, "Rune, Onyx! Where are we? I think we are in a cave by the sea!"

All the eagle hears surrounding him is his own echo calling back over and over. There is very little light left from the sun peeking through the crevices of the giant basalt columns standing tall around him. He looks around to see how he can get out noticing that the entrance to the cave is sealed off with large boulders. Escape seems impossible. He leans his head back on a nearby rock looking over again at Rune and Onyx who are peacefully sleeping on the cavern floor.

Sage sniffs the air then scratches his head curiously, "I don't know how we got out here, I think somewhere inside Mariner's Cape. Is there is no way out where we can escape?! I do not know why you two will not wake up? It must have been something you drank in that cup! Lazuli, Peony, Ember and Fifi are nowhere around, I wish I could get out of here, so they can all be found!" His echo once again reverberates the cavern cape.

Turning around Sage sees a small, cyan crab crawling toward him. As it crawls closer, he sees the translucent crab look up at him, "Good evening Mr. Bird my names Ollie, I have some good news, I hope it makes you jolly. I can tell you how to find the Phoenix of Fire, first you must call out to the Moon Mermaid to make the quest transpire. The Moon Mermaid with the Mystic Mirror which reflects all that is true, will manifest the vision needed *now* for you. Under the constellation of Cancer, you must conjure the Moon Mermaid here to give you an answer.

Her name is Azulena Aquablue, who will use this cavern wellspring to swim here right to you. She uses her Mystic Mirror for scrying, to find your friends she will look into it for spying. Showing her the future, the present and past, to help you break free of this prison at last. You must call Azulena now as the waves crash and crescendo knocks, for she lives here in this ocean oasis of giant, jagged rocks. Holding up her Mystic Mirror when lightning strikes it, ignites the night, with fiery light, to make the vision clearer. An ocean oracle of salt, sea and sand, charges the mirror she holds in her hand. An image of truth will come through, as the ladybirds lost will be revealed to you. The most important part to mention is to stand in the sand with pure intention. Then you call out Azulena, Azulena, Azulena Aquablue! Show me your vision pure and true! What is revealed in her Mystic Mirror is only to a few. The celestial sunlight beams through dark, dense clouds shining, creating on its mists a silvery lining. The reflection once again will become clearer, as the vision of truth reflects in her Mystic Mirror. Having cosmic consciousness inside her third eye as the sands of time go sifting by, holding the silver spyglass in the palm of her hand reveals a daring destiny preplanned! The Mystic Mirror knows and tells all true, you must call out now to Azulena Aquablue!"

Sage smiles, "Thank you, this is what I will do."

"Heed my advice for she lives here in paradise, deep down where the sea is cool, walk over to the pristine pool." Raising one claw he points in the direction of the dark blue salt water before the crab crawls back down a nearby rock.

Sage shakes his head as he walks to the edge of the waving water. Looking into the rows of ripples he cries out, "Azulena, Azulena, Azulena Aquablue show me your vision pure and true! I have a question I need to ask of you!"

The water begins to bubble as Azulena pops out with her long blue hair slowly emerging up from out of the calm clear water. The Moon Maiden asks, "Why have you called me here? Do you need help from my Mystic Mirror? Do you have a question to seek the reflection of total truth inside introspection?"

"I need your help first to escape from this craggy, crammed, cavernous cape, with my friends here who must awake! I've called you here to make my plea, I must know exactly where to find Ember, Fifi, Lazuli and Peony, for your Mystic Mirror to show me." Sage sits down on a rock.

Azulena holds up her circle shaped mirror and starts to chant, "I ask you Mystic Mirror clear, where is Ember? Now show me here!"

Blue and white waves of mist circulate in the silver mirrors' surface as Azulena continues, "As the mist forms within my Mystic Mirror this night, like Will-o'-the-wisps dancing in the moonlight. Spirals of stars like galaxies appear, show me where Ember is, *now* show me here!"

The colors change inside the silver mirror showing red and yellow smoke with licks of fire. Azulena gazes in the face of her Mystic Mirror and chants yet again, "Looking into my Mystic Mirror, I ask to see the vision clearer, where is the Phoenix of Fire, from Ember's glow? Where is she hiding? Where did she go?"

The answer appears in the mirror to the mermaid as she states firmly, "It's Queen Marie, I can clearly see; inside her birdcage wig, a bird of red, upon her head, perched on a Climbing Rose twig! I see satin skirts swirling by spun silken slacks, of Kings, Queens, knights, knaves, Jesters and Jacks! I see a pretty prison in a condensed space, poor Ember is in a very far place- It's a grand ballroom of ladies and gents in a dance, within a chateau castle, in the south of France! She is trapped inside the Theater of Time, looks like the year could be seventeen eighty-nine?! This majestic palace is on a cliffside at sunset, owned by a lady known as Marie Antoinette! The ocean oracle sees a portal door that opens right at midnight and closes then at four. You'll only have four hours in which to pass through;

otherwise, you have to wait until the next night to do. At the last stroke of midnight this whirlpool shall open wide to let you all go forth inside."

Sage is skeptical, "How do I find this portal door, for I have never heard of it before?"

Azulena replies, "A secret space holds this vast vortex where? inside Black Shuck Mountain it holds the portal there. The entrance is hidden by a thick forest full of Fir, fig, peach and pear. You will find the green doors up a rocky mountain stair, however to open them up you *must beware*. I see many strangers and countless dangers you two first must pass, to find the Great Grandfather Clock made of Elm, Oak, tin and brass. You must go through crimson curtains then down a long wooden hall; it is at the end, when time will bend, through the clock the floor will fall. It will tick the tock of time when its hands hit twelve, the bells will chime. Then the portal shall open up its invisible door, where you must return the same way as you came in before. Wait and watch for the clock to open wide for you to go forth inside. Look, listen and don't be late, time won't wait, by these rules you must abide."

Sage looks into her mirror wondering, "I must find my friends Lazuli and Peony too; can you please ask your Mystic Mirror so I will know what to do?"

Azulena smiles and chants once more, "Mystic Mirror that knows all true, show me Lazuli and Peony in your reflection of you!" Misty blue waves form over the face of the glass as the image appears of Lazuli and Peony still sleeping inside a gigantic, old Oak Tree. Azulena looks up, "Lazuli and Peony are asleep in the Old Hangman's Tree inside Gallows Grove is the vision that I see."

Sage looks at her with excitement, "The sound of success is what I hear, for Gallows Grove is very near! Thank you! I have one last question Azulena Aquablue, if you don't mind, I want to ask you where Fifi is since I don't have a clue?!"

106

Azulena looks back into her mirror, "Mystic Mirror, tell me true, where is Fifi? This I ask of you." The glass surface turns a gloomy gray with storm clouds gathering as it slowly reveals frightening images to the mermaid. The vision becomes clear and she sees Fifi dancing slowly with Diavolo on a cracked stone floor. Black candles glow all around the couple as a stained glass rose window appears.

Azulena is concerned, "Fifi is with a Vampire Bat wearing a silk suit made of armor, you better get there fast for he intends to harm her! He's spinning her over a tomb under the full Hunter Moon. In the old boneyard, where all the dead dwell, under a withering rose stained glass window, one with a broken church bell." Azulena turns the silver mirror toward Sage so he can see the vision too.

Sage instinctively ruffles his feathers, "I knew that bat was up to no good! He's out to destroy the whole neighborhood!"

Azulena reassures him calmly, "First, we must get your friends to arise, open the cave so you can fly free into the skies. I now command the power of a lightning bolt, to blast open this wall of rocks with one giant jolt!"

The Moon Mermaid holds up her Mystic Mirror facing the glass in front of the rocks blocking the exit. Out from the mirror comes a big bright electric charge that shoots the wall of the cave outward with a thunderous explosion. The boulders that block the entrance break and crack flying in every direction. The opening reveals the sunshine reflecting on the ocean leading out onto a sandy beach. Onyx and Rune jump to their feet quite startled by the big blast.

Rune's big eyeballs glow, "What was that? It just woke me."

Onyx rubs his eyes, "Where are we? In a cave by the sea?"

Sage stares at Azulena then looks out at the beach in amazement, "Jumping jellyfish! I sure got my wish! We must go quickly now to the Hangman's Tree, to rescue Lazuli and Peony so they can both be free!"

Out of the clear clean water Azulena hands Sage a blue bottle saying seriously, "Take this Elixir of Life from this Fountain of Youth, pour it into their mouths they will awaken to know the truth."

Sage calls out toward one of rocks joyfully, "Thank you Ollie, if you can hear me? We all have our freedom! This was meant to be!" He turns his attention back to the mermaid taking the bottle from her bowing, "Thank you so very much Azulena Aquablue, for your ocean oracle and your Mystic Mirror too! I have a gift I'd like to give, for saving our lives so we can live." Sage offers up one of his own golden feathers to the grateful mermaid.

Azulena takes the feather putting it between her pressed prayer hands, "I have a deep feeling by you birds believing determination and persistence you'll be achieving. All Birds of Paradise must unite, despite the fright of flight or fight. Do your best, upon this quest, do not be divided, have no fear, don't shed a tear, be the power united. I know you birds must go, time won't last, so get there fast, be like water go with the flow!"

Azulena does a backflip diving backwards down deep into the teal turquoise liquid. Water splashes everywhere as her opalescent scales and iridescent fin disappear back underneath the sea waters' surface. The three birdgents take off quickly through the opening up into the bright blue sky.

Onyx, Rune and Sage fly as fast as they can to Gallows Grove looking for the specific Oak Tree wrapped with a dirty, empty noose. Once they find the massive tree, the three of them frantically dig through the walls of dirt and rocks that trap Lazuli and Peony inside.

Sage waves his wings looking over at Rune and Onyx barking out orders, "We birdgents will split up, Onyx and I will fly back in time to find Ember in the theater upon the clock chime. We must find the palace of Queen Marie, to save then set our Firebird free. Try your best to awaken Lazuli and Peony, then go to the cemetery to rescue Fifi. I have been told she's with the Vampire Bat, you know, the one in the zoot zuit and fedora hat. Here's the elixir that Azulena gave me, pour it into the beaks of Lazuli and Peony, when you set them free from this tree." Sage hands Rune the blue bottle before he and Onyx fly off in the dismal direction of Black Shuck Mountain.

Rune picks up Peony and brings her out into the mossy meadow then takes Lazuli out of the old tree placing him next to her. Rune opens the blue bottle, pouring the elixir into their beaks in an attempt to wake them. Rune shakes both birds gently, only Peony opens her eyes, she sits upright and starts squawking, "I've just had the worst nightmare I've ever had! Fifi was in a graveyard crying and was very sad. I saw her trapped inside a crooked crypt covered in big black stones, while all around her in the dirt were laughing skulls and bones!"

Lazuli rises up wide eyed alert and alarmed screeches, "I too had a horrific nightmare; it's really given me quite a scare! I was surrounded by weird wolves and other misfit monsters of the night. I saw our fearless Firebird putting up a fight, went from dim lit to burning bright. She was behind bars inside a covered cage, her eyes were glowing and growing with rage. Her light fading fast inside a cage made of lead; I was struggling to get her out before she fell down dead!"

Rune replies in a strictly, "We all must work together as a team, to figure out this sinister scheme!"

Peony glances over at Lazuli, "That Cherry Wine was much too bitter it needed sugar cane."

Lazuli shakes his fluffy feathers, "I think we were given a drink of Hemlock and Henbane."

Rune spins his head in a circle, "Someone's been wort cunning and wild crafting? Most likely it was those two crow clowns!"

Peony starts to stand up, "I'm afraid that Vampire Bat followed her sound, remember at the ball, she was nowhere to be found."

Lazuli replies angerly, "They spiked the punch then off they flew, I bet they also bird napped Ember too!"

Rune taps his foot in frustration, "A trick disguised as a treat to put on a show, come on let's hurry, I'm ready to go!"

Peony rubs at her forehead, "I think my nightmare is a premonition from my female intuition."

Runes eyes grow wide and glow bright, "I know where she is at, in the cemetery with that no-good Vampire Bat!"

Lazuli's anger grows along with his feathers, "THAT BIG, BAD, BAT, BIRD-NAPPED FIFI! WE BETTER FIND HER FAST, BEFORE HE MAKES A MEAL OF HER LIKE HE TRIED WITH ME IN THE PAST!"

Peony has a worried look on her feathered face, "Where are Sage and Onyx? They didn't just disappear?"

Rune flaps his wings, "Peony please have no fear, very soon they will all be here. Hurry! Let's get to the graveyard quick, there's a Vampire villain I want to kick!"

Rune and Peony fly off as Lazuli runs quickly along the ground following right behind them.

Sage and Onyx are flying toward the middle of Black Shuck Mountain hearing the faint sound of a player piano way in the distance. Their concentration is shattered when a sharp rock passes by between the two birds. Bonard and Buster have emerged from their hiding spot, hidden behind a giant fig tree. The goose goons begin shooting stones at them from their slingshots. Sage and Onyx are forced to fly in opposite directions to miss being hit by the flying rocks. One rock flew into the tip of Sages right wing so he turns to follow Onyx who flies frantically around Sage getting the goose goons both to fire their sharp stones at him. Both birds glide down to stop and hide inside a nearby tree trunk. They keep quiet as the sneaky geese look for them below with their slingshots at the ready, aiming to shoot. Sage and Onyx blend in perfectly with the wide stump as they are forced to wait for hours, not saying a word until the two geese goons give up.

Onyx whispers, "We only have a small pocket of time; we've got one hour left until the clock will chime,"

Sage whispers back, "Tables have turned, now *we're their* prey. We have to make a break for it so we can get away. I'll meet you at the clock if we have to split, ok?"

Onyx nods in agreement before they both bolt up and out of the stump then into the canopy of leaves. The many leaves rustle allowing the two gangster geese to catch sight of them in the distance being swallowed by the bending branches. Bonard and Buster fly forward swiftly.

Bernard screams, "HEY YOU! BIRD OF PREY! CATCHING YOU WILL INCREASE MY PAY!"

Buster screams louder, "WHAT ARE YOU GOING TO SAY?! YOU TRYING TO RUIN OUR DAY?!"

All the while the two gangster geese continue to fire the jagged rocks from their slingshots stopping every so often to pick them back up from off the ground.

Onyx dodges another flying rock, "Good thing these old, dirty buzzards can't aim, last thing we need is a wing to go lame."

Sage flies swiftly in the opposite direction saying, "Talk about your wild goose chase; we *really* need to pick up our pace!"

The brave birds hurry over the thick forest then up into tree tops. Sage spots the two green doors carved into the side of the massive mountain. They swoop down to stand straight in front of the old, ornately carved green doors that will lead them inside the Lucky Ducky Club. Opening the doors both birds' step into the plush gambling hall where there are numerous ducks shooting dice and geese playing cards at many tables. A few goose gals are walking around with drinks on their trays, others are serving flapper fowl who are sitting with their birdgent companions. All the players and patrons in the club stop their gambling games to look over at Sage and Onyx silently. Instinctively some of the gangster geese and dangerous ducks grab stones and slingshots from out of their belts and coat pockets.

"Now wait there just a minute birdgents, put your slingshots away, ladybirds, we are here to work as part of the play. We've been hired to perform here too, a *special* comedy just for you! We are just a couple of comedy clowns hired to pantomime, so we'll only be here a short time. Excuse us as we make our way to the dressing room, start playing the piano there fellow, we'll be out here real soon!"

The dapper ducks and dandy dames are distracted once more by the piano player as they watch two showgirls enter on stage wearing black and blue outfits. The fancy flappers continue drinking their Elderberry wine as the goose gals pass out Lazy Daisy gin juleps. The groups of greedy ganders go back to their gambling games while guzzling sap rum and apple ale. Sage and Onyx proceed quickly through the crimson curtains through props of painted walls and stacked boxes through the dressing rooms backstage until the find the hidden hall. At the very end of the long hallway standing straight against the far wall was the unusually painted carefully carved Great Grandfather Clock.

One goose gal at the bar turns around suspiciously, "There's something familiar about those guys, I think,"

The bartender pouring two drinks at once shouts, "THERE'S A PECKING ORDER HERE DOLLY, SERVE FRANK HERE HIS DRINK!"

Just then Bonard and Buster throw open the front doors, rushing into the club and run cautiously across the room. Bonard yells loudly, "Have you seen an eagle and raven we've been trying to shoot?! They're a couple of thieves come to steal our loot!"

All the ducks and geese fly up out of their seats and make a run for backstage going after the two silent strangers. Sage and Onyx can hear them approaching, honking and quacking angrily behind them. Spotting the clock down the hallway Sage and Onyx fly as fast as they can to open the clocks portal door.

In the middle of many paintings, boxes, props and costumes sits a gigantic Great Grandfather Clock. It has four etched glass doors, two on each side and two in the middle that open outward. It's made out of polished Oak wood with carved leaves and painted flowers on each side. The large face of the glass is opaque pearl with black Roman numerals decorating it. There is a golden sun and silver moon on each side with a sprinkle of sparkling stars. Onyx opens both glass doors as a cloud of mist swirls a spiral around him and Sage. The pendulum stops swinging letting both birds enter inside, then they disappear encased within a dense fog. The angry gangsters reach the Great Grandfather Clock before Buster opens the doors to reveal only its golden pendulum swinging back and forth. Splitting up the gangsters continue to look around for the two strangers with their slingshots ready to fire.

Sage and Onyx have fallen in through a moving tunnel of mist then suddenly appear inside a puffy white cloud floating in a sunny sky. The two birds glide off into the setting sunset in the theater of time.

They look down to see miles of trees with houses and dairy farms filled with cows and goats. An old wooden mill is churning a rushing river next to a barn, stable and acres of citrus orchards. They fly on, past majestic mansions, with ladies in hoopskirt ballgowns of bright colors, walking with their suited gentlemen. They see endless rows of fruit trees, berry bushes and different colors of flowers with herb gardens surrounded by many plantations of cotton. They continue to fly past old western towns filled with covered wagons and poor prairie people. Native warriors and Indian chiefs are riding on horseback toward teepee villages across vast plains filled with horses and bison.

Both birds stay on course passing chicken coops and crops of corn, various vegetables and lots of grazing goats and shepherds shearing sheep. Crossing rivers, lakes and finally the ocean, the birds fly over Spanish Galleons firing their cannons. Onyx points his wing at the glass glaciers of blue ice and arctic animals climbing the frozen white mountain. Penguins and Polar bears play in the swirling snow while walrus watch and seal's swim.

Flying on past many fishing boats and a few canoes are towering emerald islands with an active volcano surrounded by palm trees in the sparkling sand. There are many men fishing using their nets in the large lagoons catching fish. Others are displaying their catch of the day on the sandy shore selling their share. The two birds fly on as the ocean goes out for miles kissing the dusk as it turns into dawn on the distant horizon.

Onyx is starting to get tired, "Do you have a bird's-eye view? Are we there yet?"

Sage yawns as he sees the last rays of the sun vanish, "With an image like *that*, I wouldn't forget."

CHAPTER 20

Marie and Mirette

After what seems like hours Sage and Onyx arrive at the noble palace sitting on the side of a cliff above rough roaring waves crashing against the big boulders below. The brave birds fly onto the nearest tree to perch and rest after their long journey. After a while of exploring the castle grounds they notice an orange orchard surrounded by a lined tapestry terrace and various vines of green grapes. The heads of the citrus topiary trees are pruned perfectly into shaped spheres. Along the winding paths they see brightly colored flower beds, rose bushes and fountains with human marble statues. Finally, both birds perch on a lemon tree branch outside in the open courtyard where guests are meeting and mingling. Onyx and Sage are close enough to look into a wide window watching for Queen Marie.

Inside a spacious pink parlor room adjusting her natural hair into a form fitting cotton cap is the Queen. She is sitting in front of an imprinted white vanity chair with a round framed mirror and clawed feet. Marie applies her cosmetics of pink lipstick, red rouge and fine white powder to her face. Her lady in waiting Mirette, hands Marie an ornately carved jewelry box which Marie opens to take out her earrings and matching necklace to put on. Mirette makes final adjustments by using a white talc and powder puff to pat the wig she intends for the Queen to wear. The overwhelming cloud of dry dust has awakened Ember who is locked inside a birdcage within her white wig, she can't help but cough and sneeze.

Mirette notices the movement in the cage and asks curiously, "Is that a real live bird?"

Marie looks up in between the bars at Ember sitting on the silver swing. Marie is surprised, "Oh my Mirette, a ruby red bird? It looks like a cardinal."

Mirette holds out the work of art proudly in her hands. She presents the white wig to Marie that has a beautiful birdcage wrapped inside the white hair covered in roses. Mirette places the wig on Marries head then proceeds to place on her crown when they both notice Ember trying to stand up in the birdcage. Ember blinks on and off trying to ignite her fire feathers. This amuses Marie so she giggles while Mirette continues to pin her crown to her wig. After the two ladies finish making themselves pretty with powder puffs and perfume, they walk out of the parlor chamber together and back into the grand hall. Marie passes a giant, gold, full-length filigree mirror in the hallway, she stops to admire herself in her pale pink evening gown. Seeing her image, she glances once again at Ember flickering between the birdcage bars. She looks over at her lady in waiting who is looking at the flaming firebird.

Mirette giggles, "Isn't that romantic?"

Marie wonders as she looks at Ember, "Who would do such a silly thing?"

Mirette flutters her fan in her face, "Why a secret admirer of course, it must be a gift!"

Marie locks eyes with Mirette, "It might be a joke."

Mirette shakes her head side to side, "Oh no, I don't think so my lady, all of us have someone in our lives who secretly adores us."

"Well, I hope he shows up tonight and asks me to dance, after all I'm not getting any younger." Marie admires her face in the mirror.

"You my Queen are the bell of the ball, many men are going to ask you to dance, you may have your pick of plenty a gentleman here who will want your hand." Marie turns around to look at Mirette who reaches for her hand.

Marie squeezes Mirette's' hand back and begins to lead her to the bubbling fountain sitting on the dessert table, "Come Mirette, let us eat cake and drink champagne."

Marie and Mirette continue to walk across the room, entering into the baroque ballroom together. A French horn player on each side of the door blows a fanfare announcing the Queens arrival. All the ladies and gentlemen turn around to stare and smile at the natural beauty of the made-up monarch. Marie watches as their eyes become fixated at the live bird glowing a dull red inside the birdcage. Ember has fully awakened to see the costumed humans who are all wearing many masks of different kinds of animals staring at her. There are wild wolves, bearded bears, high-horned deer, festive foxes and racy rabbits. Ember looks over at Mirette, who has a Schooner ship rocking on her waves of baby blue curls. Mirette's large eyes are now looking at her too from behind her prison of lead bars.

Frightened, Ember attempts to escape once again by making her frazzled feathers spark fire. The ladies walk over to the champagne fountain with an ice sculpture of Cupid holding up his bow and arrow. They each grab a glass as Ember sadly realizes that the cage is made of steel and lead making her efforts useless. She begins to screech in frustration louder and louder until she reached a pitch where it shattered the two ladies' glasses. A few men came over to check on them if they got hurt, fortunately for the giggling girls the shards of splinters end up on the floor. Mirette quickly grabs two more glasses off of the table and hands one to Marie. They both fill them up with champagne at the fountain before clinking them together.

Mirette holds up her glass, "A toast for your happiness; may this evening show you how, even if you don't find Mister Right tonight, you may meet Mister Right now."

Marie holds her glass against Mirette's, "Here is a toast to finding my King tonight with a love that will last forever; a gentleman to take my hand who is tall, rich, trim and clever." Marie smiles sipping her champagne.

Marie shakes her head side to side, "I don't plan on getting my heart broken again; it's going to take some time before it will mend."

The two ladies clink glasses once again, "Well, I've waited all through my twenties and now that I'm thirty-two, I better meet someone soon, or I shall end up an old spinster with you." Marie smiles before taking a sip of the bitter bubbles. She notices many men and women around the ballroom looking at her in admiration.

Mirette announces, "This is Queen Marie's night to find her faithful King, he can be short or tall, big or small. You gentle-men are not allowed to brawl, only a battle of brains allowed for our beautiful Bell of the Ball!"

The elegant women walk together across the ballroom to the display of scrumptious selections of cakes and cookies decorated with fruits and flowers. Men in elaborate costumes follow behind them crossing the floor admiring their beauty while trying to ask them for a dance.

Marie and Mirette stop in front of a Teak table full of fine foods. Mirette sings shyly, "Tonight you are the Bell of the Ball; some advice from your good friend, a toast in France, that romantic dance, will never come again. After all my Bell of the Ball is in the prime of her years, it seems by now she's been through it all, laughter and many shed tears. Enjoy this day, for come what may, every moment that has been, each smiling face, each warm embrace, for it will never come again."

As if waiting for a turn the fine gentlemen each sing a line to Marie:

Charles starts, "Bravo to your party my Dear, I hear you throw them four times a year?"

Fredrick is next, "Why my Queen I do declare, is that a live bird there, that's in your hair?"

Edward chimes, "Look at that fabulous fabric! Who designed your gown?"

Thomas croons, "Did you design it yourself or get it at Abagail's downtown?"

Charles resonates, "You are an elegant, exquisite beauty, the Bell of the Ball!"

Fredrick buzzes, "May I send you a pigeon soon to give you a call?"

Edward warbles, "May you please join me for a walk in the garden here?"

Thomas intones, "It would be my honor for your first dance, my dear."

All the guests in the ballroom sing out, harmonizing together: "After all, the Bell of the Ball is in the prime of her years; it seems by now she's been through it all- Laughter and many shed tears, enjoy this day, for come what may, every moment that has been; a sunset walk, a sunrise talk, for it will never come again."

Charles carols, "Your style is so Rococo- I must know who does your hair?"

Fredrick bellows, "Every eye is on you- See how the Duke and Dutchess stare?

Edward squeals, "The shoes that match your dress are perfectly dyed!"

Thomas tunes, "Come dance with me my Queen, with your graceful stride!"

Charles whines, "Don't be shy my love and hide behind your fan."

Fredrick fidgets, "If you're looking for a husband, look no further, I'm your man."

Edward boasts, "I own my own business of imports and exports too."

Thomas regales, "I was voted most handsome in the year seventeen seventy-two!"

All the guests now stand around Marie and Mirette and sing out: "After all the Bell of the Ball is in the prime of her years, it seems by now you've been through it all, the laughter and many shed tears, enjoy this day, for come what may, every moment that has been; holidays at home, summer walks alone, for it will never come again."

Marie sings back to her guests, "To name me as the Bell of the Ball, the most beautiful of them all, will fade away, like a passing day, a Rosebud to blossom and fall. As my petals shall drop and decay, no matter what they may say, I will remember January through December, to be blessed by what is pleasant, realize and fantasize, there's no gift quite like the present!"

Charles declares, "Your make up is so pure against your skin like milk."

Fredrick falters, "You are the best dressed lady here, with your dress of- Satin silk?"

Edward points out, "You sparkle like a diamond mine, with that necklace and those rings!"

Thomas trills, "Perfect stones for a flawless lady in dazzling drop earrings."

Charles begs, "Where have you been my Queen all my life?"

Fredrick laughs nervously, "I know you will make the perfect wife."

Edward laments, "The scent of your perfume, I must know its name."

Thomas serenades, "Marry me my love and your life will never be the same."

All the guests pair off as couples and begin dancing around the ballroom while singing: "After all, the Bell of the Ball, will reign Queen till the end of her days, in the prime of her life, make a proper wife, so love her now and always. Enjoy the now, and you'll see how, every moment that has been, each touch you miss, each tender kiss, for it will never come again."

Mirette pierces the air, "The Bell of the Ball, is the most beautiful of them all!"

Marie sings softly, "I'm impressed Mirette, at your etiquette; I'm so happy you are my friend, I will enjoy this time, it is all mine, for it will never come again."

Charles and Fredrick extend their arms to Marie and Mirette walking arm in arm onto the massive dance floor with other couples who all start dancing a waltz to the beat of the classical orchestra.

"Just how long is this dance?" Onyx fights off a yawn.

"We have to wait until we get our chance," Sage reminds him.

Sage and Onyx are still perched out on the branch of an orange tree growing inside the courtyard. Both birds are looking through the window for the Queen wearing the birdcage wig on her head. After a while the two birds fly around the manicured gardens looking into every window. Thomas takes Marie's arms on the dance floor before he escorts her out into the courtyard. They both walk through rows of roses and across the fragrant flowers to sit privately on a bench by a flowing fountain while Marie feeds vanilla cake to him laughing while sipping champagne.

Marie asks within a softspoken tone, "Can you see us repeating this in the heat of another midsummer?"

Thomas responds fondly kissing her dainty hand, "Yes Marie, In mid-June on our wedding day."

Marie laughs again, "wedding day? If that's a proposal I will say yes." She clinks her glass with his and drinks.

Sage finally spots Marie, "*There! There* she is Onyx do you see Queen Marie? Sitting with that gentleman underneath that tree!" Sage points his wing down toward the kissing couple. Onyx looks down to see them and notices the flowing fountain.

"Now I see the Queen, how do we take the birdcage without being seen?" Onyx looks around the courtyard at all the pretty people still mingling about talking and laughing while playing games of Chess or Checkers.

"I will swoop down swiftly and pull the birdcage off the Queen." Sage flaps his wide wings together.

"Very well then, I will distract them by singing a song; you grab the birdcage since you are so strong." Onyx puffs out his chest and ruffles his feathers before he glides down to land in the water beside them. He begins splashing around inside the marble fountain placed next to the flirting couple. Thomas and Marie watch the raven nearby as he trebles and tweets while enjoying his bird bath.

Marie giggles again, "Well it certainly *is not* a dove."

Thomas smiles touching her cheek, "A romantic raven has come serenading sonnets of poems and prose."

The cuddling couple continue to watch Onyx sing as Sage swoops down and pulls the birdcage wig right off Marie's head making her appear bald. He flies off up into the sky with it in his talons as Marie begins to scream, grabbing her head where her real hair is hidden under a coiffure cap.

Any of the guests outside observing the moment Marie's wig is removed by the Bird of Prey starts clapping thinking it is all part of a planned event so they yell out, "Bravo! Bravo!

Thinking quickly the Queen wipes her tears and starts laughing while bowing and blowing kisses to her small appreciative audience, "Oui, Oui, Merci, merci beaucoup!"

Sage soars with the birdcage firmly in his grasp as he makes his way up into the hills with Onyx by his side. He gently places it on the green grass and begins to pull the metal bars apart with his giant talons freeing the Phoenix.

Ember dusts off the remaining talc powder as she steps out of the bent-up bars frowning, "I'm grateful to you both now I have to go release my rage, it *was* those malicious magpies that locked me up inside this cage!"

Sage steps out in front of her, "We must fly quickly back to rescue Fifi, we know where she is at, to save her from the clutches of that vicious Vampire Bat!"

Sage, Onyx and Ember fly back from the way in which they came until the three birds hear the familiar chime of Great Grandfather clock. With a whoosh, the time portal opens allowing a glint of light from the clock's pendulum to be seen swinging left to right in the distance inside a thick cloud. The birds fly faster to reach the clocks glistening doors.

"I can hear the clang of the bells' chime, that will lead us where we were back in time!" Onyx exclaims.

"I can see the pendulum of where the clock swings, beware Ember, of all those ding-a-lings!" Sage explains.

"Oh no, they best beware of *me*; *they're the ones* that will want to flee!" Ember replies her eyes starting to glow really red.

Sage opens the glass doors in front of the pendulum where they arrive back inside the Lucky Ducky Club. No time has passed as the dangerous ducks and gangster geese are still roaming about everywhere looking for them. When they finally do spot Sage, Onyx and Ember they prepare their slingshots, aiming to shoot at them. At full speed Ember flies down the hall, her eyes glowing an intense red, she's hot under the feathers like a Tiki-Torch, Ember over takes the stage with her wings extended, brilliantly blazing.

Ember screams out, "What's good for the goose is good for the gander after all! Hey boys how would you like to catch *my* fireball?" She puts her wings together in front of her creating flames between them. Her wings move back and forth until they manifest a burning ball. One after the other she starts throwing the fireballs at the gangsters which they try to avoid. The fireballs catch the stage, curtains and tables on fire. A few fireballs end up behind the bar forcing bottles and glasses to break. The moonshine fueled flames shoot higher and higher crawling up to the ceiling. Now the flustered fowl are forced to give up pursuit and rush to get buckets of water. They run back and forth honking and quacking with feathers flying all over the place. Sage, Onyx and Ember escape easily past the pandemonium and out the door of the not-so-Lucky Ducky.

"Ember! What an impressive attack!" Sage can't help but smile.

"Yeah, she didn't cut them any slack," Onyx replies laughing.

"It was just like water off a ducks' back," Ember nods in agreement.

CHAPTER 21

Italian Bat

Diavolo is dancing with Fifi, spinning her around and around inside the longstanding, gothic church forgotten by time. The dilapidated structure has broken bricks, empty rooms and shattered stained glass windows. The silence is interrupted by the sound of an old organ being played by a large rat in the chapel. The main alter is lit up by many black candles illuminating all the religious relics.

"I just want to sweep you off your feet, my sweet; trust me, I'm looking out for your best interest, you're a damsel in distress, I'm a knight in armored vest. Let's tiptoe through the tombstones tonight, everything is going to be alright. I have a song for you I want to sing; don't worry you won't feel a thing." Diavolo holds her closer to him.

Fifi yawns as she attempts to keep her eyes open, "You have a lot of nerve, venomous vipers like you always get what they deserve," Fifi replies sleepily, "Dancing with you I'm neither impressed or inspired, in fact all this dancing is making me terribly tired."

Diavolo keeps Fifi in his clutches holding her securely to him whispering, "Fall asleep my luscious lady, as I sing my lullaby, dance off into a dream, then I shall say good-bye."

"Look, you are making me cry; everything *you* promised has been one big lie," Fifi weeps.

Diavolo continues to spin Fifi around singing to her, "The breath of death whispers in your ear, while this woman of smoke draws very near. Now that the Blood Moon has risen, how she's created her own prison. I see into your rosy eyes a captivating stare; your haunting cryptic calm speaks to me in prayer. Hearts have wings through soulless eyes, behind a feather mask we all wear a disguise- Why would I ever harm her? Rumors are whispered through empty

suits of armor? Cloaked figures loom with torches lit
aflame, hearing in sickly silence the calling of your name.
Stone cold walls hard inside a labyrinth is lost, among the
tall black barren trees covered in winters frost. Beneath
the chessboard floor is where we play our games, the walls
have ears, the walls have eyes through staring picture
frames. The castle is a prison; the Queen is but a slave,
in her golden ballroom inside the center of the maze. Lost
in a hall of mirrors of gold leaf filigree, you can't find
your way out of the darkness here without me. Hidden
doorways lead to nowhere, rooms are left unseen, all the
windows are locked shut inside the castle of the Queen.
Dancing with the Devil a harlequin and a horse, in an array
of swirling bubbles, as nighttime takes its course. For on
the stroke of midnight, you'll be swaying in the spotlight-
Halloween is a holiday where all is not what it may seem,
so go ahead, think of your bed, fall asleep and dream.
Fluffy feathers adorn her face above her beak blood red, as
she twirls around, to the sound of morbid music by the
dead. A big, bad, bat came to greet her and into his arms
she fell, hypnotizing, mesmerizing, under my supernatural
spell. We'll dance to Macabre Music until the witching
hour, then I'll take you up the spire winding tower. The
quiet Queen will be a simple slave, to be trapped in a
dungeon from cradle to grave. This masquerade is an
illusion of confusion to deceive, once you climb these
catacombs you will never leave. I'll watch your color fade,
to become a paler shade, this evening is for *me* to keep,
close your eyes, as time flies, as I sing you to sleep.
This castle is your prison, your remaining days, among the
burning candles of ghastly gloomy haze. Bewitching you
can't talk or scream, close your eyes, to starry skies,
fall asleep and dream. Feel the wind it whispers beware, go
against me if *you* dare- I know you can hear it, sounds of
ghostly ghouls screaming in scary spooky spirit. Dance with
me my Queen across this chessboard floor; I'm your knight
in shining armor, the one you've been waiting for. This
castle crypt where the wind whispers our names, the walls
have ears, the walls have eyes, through staring picture
frames. Do you find me entertaining? Obstinate? Obscene?
Close your eyes, for your demise, fall asleep and dream."

Fifi can no longer fight his hypnotic harmony and falls to sleep reluctantly in Diavolo's fuzzy arms. He grabs her tightly and flies off with her to the top of the church tower. Diavolo laughs to himself, "looks like Diavolos delusions of grandeur can only increase, you my fine flamingo are my marvelous masterpiece!"

"Peony look; there they go! There's Diavolo with Fifi in tow! Looks like Fifi is clearly in danger, being carried off by that vile, shadow stranger!" Rune points his wing toward the tall top spire.

"You are smarter, stronger, shrewder and divinely glorious, go after them and you will be victorious," Peony clasps her wings together.

They watch the Vampire Bat and French flamingo disappear into the darkness. Diavolo holds Fifi closer, looking into her face as she lies listless in his sharp curled claws. He hisses, "You have to admit I was slick; I give you this trick, *you* give me a treat, for my main course is *your* life force, it's both savory and sweet."

Diavolo prepares to bite her neck, moving ever closer with his mouth open. Suddenly, he gets knocked hard against a wall by Rune and loses his grasp on Fifi. Rune seizes the moment, picking Fifi up quickly. He flies out through the top of the open tower. Getting up slowly Diavolo shakes the cobwebs off, before limping over to the window see if he can catch sight of them.

Unlike the garden glen the chilly, gusty wind here moans. In the dark distance a pack of wild wolves' howl. He looks over at an old tombstone that reads ANNE CHANTED with a carved stone face on a bust staring back at him. Looking around he sees numerous graves with many statues, candles and flowers. Stepping up his pace skipping toward the tall tower talking to himself Lazuli quietly questions, "Is that wolves that are near? howling here? I better hide in the church since it's death I fear." Quite frightened, a shaking Lazuli runs as fast as he can through the cemetery surrounded by mounds of moss, twisted tress and warn-down gravesites.

Finally, he sees lights flickering inside the crumbling church. Following the path by the light he finally stands before old weather-beaten wooden beamed doors underneath the withering rose stained glass window. Peering down from the ruins of the massive building are gargoyle goblins and grotesque gremlins growling at him. Trembling he says to himself, "Now why did I agree? What is wrong with *me*? It's so dark in here I can't even see! This is the *last place* I want to be. I will not fear, I cannot fly, Oh dear, I don't really want to die!"

Lazuli enters through the decrepit doors as he looks around to see many melting candles in holders made from smiling skulls. The grimacing gazes show their teeth as if laughing at him. Lazuli tries to comfort himself, "Don't want to wake the dead; don't want to be the next head! Excuse me, but I have to flee, if you'll allow, I think I'll just be going now."

Exiting the old church, he shuts the doors and turns around just in time to see Rune and Peony out in the distance laying Fifi down near a crusty crypt. Rune seems out of breath and sitting down to rest while Peony attends to Fifi. Neither notices an enormous black figure moving closer and closer in dark shadows toward them from a far distance. Lazuli's eyes grow big when he spots an advancing arachnid made from corn cobs covered in cotton. Large wooden wispy legs are crawling silently and stealthy over granite gravestones. He gathers his bravery to warn his friends frantically screaming as loud as he can, "LOOK OUT FROM BEHIND, IT'S SOME KIND OF FRANKENFOODSTIEN!"

Rune and Peony turn around to see a giant eight-legged machine made to look like a Goliath bird-eating tarantula moving straight for them. Rune picks up Fifi just as Ember, Onyx and Sage appear in the sky flying over to join them. Ember creates and heaves fireballs at the monstrous mechanism catching one of its legs on fire. This forces it to turn around and try to crawl back into the forest blazing brightly. Soon all of its legs are engulfed in flames as it stops to burn in the middle of the graveyard. Unexpectedly, kernels of corn begin popping out in all directions one after the other. Magnolia and Merlot unlock a hidden hatch from the underbelly of the fake spider they were operating together. The magpies hurry to hide in the surrounding shadows blending in with the thick, dark forest. Ember tries to find them, using her wings like torches, however they manage to remain hidden in silence.

Diavolo is still peering out of the tower window, he glares as he watches the magpies disappear into the thick foliage. He shakes his bat wings at them crying out, "Hey You chickens! I know why you crossed the road there; you want to go lay an egg? I'll find you two in a pair!"

Diavolo's eyes narrow as he notices Rune, Onyx and Sage swiftly approaching him from the sky. He flees and flies out of the window as fast as he can in an attempt to escape their talons of torment. Rune purses after the bloodthirsty bat, who is not fast enough for the bird of prey who grabs him in mid-air with his talons. The owl swoops down swiftly bringing him into the graveyard with a hard landing. They both tumble across the ground together kicking up dust. Sage and Onyx fly closer to join Rune and Diavolo as the wrestle on the ground.

Diavolo looks down at his jacket and as he starts to brush himself off screaming, "DAMN-IT SON OF A WITCH THAT REALLY HURT! LOOK AT ME! I'M COVERED IN DIRT! YOU BEST HAVE LOTS OF LOOT CAUSE NOW YOU OWE ME A NEW SUIT!"

Sage and Onyx fly over and grab Diavolo by his bat wings while Rune removes the belt, "Well Mister Mastermind bat, you really thought you would get away with that?!"

Sage flies over to face Diavolo, "WHEN YOU BIRDNAPPED FIFI I ALMOST GAVE UP HOPE, NOW I'LL SEE TO IT THAT YOU'LL BE AT THE END OF YOUR ROPE!"

Onyx grips Diavolos' wings tighter, "He never realized that he'd get caught. Steal away with Fifi that's what he thought!"

Rune proceeds to use the belt to tie Diavolo's wings tightly behind his back so Diavolo cannot free himself to fly away. Sage carefully gives Fifi a few drops of Eternal Elixir from the blue bottle. Slowly she begins to wake up, opening and rubbing at her eyes. Fifi smiles when she sees Diavolo tied up and hears the chirpy chattering from her fellow flock.

Sage yells at Diavolo, "YOU REALLY ARE A DISPICABLE, DETESTABLE, DISCUSTING DISGRACE! YOU WILL *NEVER* BE ABLE TO SHOW YOUR FACE!"

Peony pipes up, "*He* has to be imprisoned, *he* cannot be free! Let's take *him* to Gallows Grove and *LOCK HIM UP* in the old Oak tree!"

Rune tugs on the belt making sure it's secure, "When we find those magpies, we'll stick them in there too, we saw the direction in which they flew!"

Lazuli crosses his wings mocking Diavolo, "Looks like your mad-pie crooks have caused you to get caught!"

Sage shakes one of his wing feathers in Diavolos direction scolding, "The purpose in life is to value the lessons you're taught."

Runes eyes glow big and bright while angerly staring at Diavolo, "You are not to be trusted since there is no honor among thieves."

Lazuli smiles sarcastically, "Like a rat stuck in a trap, there is no such thing as free cheese."

Ember flares up her fire feathers, "I Ember *now* decree, THE *BIG BAD BAT* will be taken to the old Oak Tree!"

Sage glares at the bat, "Well it looks like you're finally out of luck!"

Peony laughs as she teases, "*You* have become the laughing stock of Phantom Island and *all* of Black Shuck!"

Lazuli quips quickly, "You're lucky to be a live chicken rather than a dead duck!"

Fifi is shocked and softspoken, "You *really* are quite strange and very deranged. You caused my chance at romance to be rearranged."

Diavolo replies back to her with his wicked smile, "That might be true, *even* coming from *you*, however, I cannot be changed."

Fifi flails her wings into the air, "How dare you trick me! *All* you said was *so* untrue, the only thing *you've* managed to do is make a *fool* of you!"

"Don't blame me; it wasn't my plan you see. Now, I have to admit-it" Diavolo shakes his head and his voice goes low, "The real truth here, is that the butler did it."

Rune has heard enough; he picks Diavolo up in his sharp talons leading the way for all the birds to follow behind him. The Birds of Paradise fly in formation as they head back to Gallows Grove. They swoop down before stopping to put the Vampire Bat inside the Hangman's Tree. The feathered friends work together to move boulders, rocks and large branches building a solid wall while leaving a small opening as a window.

Fifi asks curiously, "We will have to feed him worms, won't we?"

Sage replies firmly, "There are plenty of insect pests to eat inside that tree,"

Lazuli laughs sarcastically, "Good, he can have those stinging ants to eat!"

Onyx remains irritated, "That's what he gets for being a liar and a cheat!"

Peony boasts proudly, "I should have listened to *my* hunch; it *was* those wicked Magpies that spiked the punch!"

Ember nods happily, "Let's just be grateful we are all safe and sound, we've learned our lesson, what comes around goes a around."

Lazuli motions for the other birds to follow him holding the two food baskets, "Speaking of things to eat, follow me my feathered friends here's bee tea and tarts for a treat!"

The sun begins to rise on the horizon as Magnolia and Merlot burst out of a pile of dead leaves laughing.

Magnolia grabs Merlot's wing saying softly, "Your super spider was the *most* magnificent invention yet, next time you'll do even better I bet."

Merlot replies dryly, "I'm just glad we got away with that. I wonder where they hid the dirty Dingbat?"

Magnolia squints her eyes, "When we find him, we'll blame those bird-brains for the attack, have them to distract, that will get those goose goons off our back!"

Merlot looks into Magnolias' big black eyes flirting, "Come my beautiful doe eyed pet; I'll show you an afternoon you will never forget. Just you and I with the wind and the sky. We will retrieve our treehouse before the next rain, in *our* own food forest of fruits, nuts and grain."

The two magpies fly off together, eventually gliding over Gallows Grove. As they make their way over the towering trees, they hear Diavolo screeching and screaming. Magnolia and Merlot lock eyes sharing a glance perplexed.

The End?

www.pansfloraworld.com

If you enjoyed this book, please leave a review. Have a question or comment, I would appreciate receiving it also!

After reading this it should be of little surprise that author J.J. Adams makes her home in Hawaii. Where she has already stated she intends to return to Pansflorawood Glen, again. Though in the meantime she invites you to check out her other work!

Aloha, toot-a-loo!

Made in the USA
Middletown, DE
04 May 2024

53844408R00077